JANE AND THE MONSTER (PART 2)

MONSTERS OF THE MOUNT MOORHEAD
BOOK TWO

SOPHIA SMUT

CHAPTER

ONE

I peel my eyes open and the piercing light slices through my consciousness like a knife. I clench my eyes shut again but the intensity of discomfort only increases, and soon I am left with a splitting headache. So I lie as still as I can, feeling the luxuriously soft sheets contour to my body. The only sound and movement come from my struggling breaths. When I manage to loosen the shackles of the sheets with my right foot, I open my eyes one more time, blinking involuntarily in order to adjust to the changing brightness before me. I keep taking long pools of air, telling myself that everything is going to be all right and I don't need to panic. It's the breathing exercise that stuck with me since college.

I find myself in a dark, eerie room with gothic features that feels so surreal, it's as if I'm dreaming. Torches burn at the corners of the room, revealing countless artifacts, each casting an uncanny glow around the space. My skin crawls with fear as I look at the walls and spot a distorted painting of a dining hall, while strange vases line the shelf to my left.

Worse yet, I'm completely naked and vulnerable in this unfamiliar room. Pulling the sheets around me, I tremble as my eyes search for an escape route that doesn't seem to exist. I have this strange feeling of déjà vu, as though this has happened before, which is impossible because I'd swear this is by far the strangest place I have ever been in. What I remember is climbing the mountain after speaking to my friend Dorothy, but everything after that is lost in a brain fog.

A maelstrom of chaotic thoughts races through my mind. My heart pounds in my chest, as if trying to escape, while the walls of the room seem to close in around me. My throat tightens, making it difficult to breathe, and my vision blurs as I blindly grapple with the sheets, which cling to my sweat-drenched body like a second skin. Suddenly, with a thunderous crash, I lunge from the bed in a desperate attempt to escape this tormenting nightmare. A sharp pain pierces through me as I hit the floor, and I am left feeling weak and vulnerable. Nevertheless, I know I must pull myself together, hoping the door is unlocked.

As I groan in agony, a sharp, searing pain radiates from my throat, causing me to clutch at it reflexively. With trembling hands and shaky knees, I try to get off the ground, but before I can even sit up, the door to my right suddenly bursts open. I lose my balance and slam hard onto the floor again, stunned momentarily by the impact. Struggling to push myself upright, I can barely comprehend what I'm seeing as three menacing, naked figures step into the room. Their pairs of horns, tails, and wild, shiny eyes are all fixed on me, and I realize that I'm seeing real monsters in the flesh, while my mind keeps telling me that this should be impossible.

I scream in terror, backing away toward the wall as I take in their bizarre appearance. The intensity of their stares penetrates my skin like a hot needle being driven into my flesh. They are hideous and small, but also largely built at the same time. What shocks me the most is the fact that none of them seems to be wearing any clothes.

"Stay back! Stay away!" I shout, scuttling to a corner of the room. I plaster myself to the wall, hoping to stay as far away as possible from the three monsters. My breathing becomes shallow, and my skin feels hypersensitive as panic starts to take over.

Despite my distress, I brandish my fist at the three strange creatures in front of me. Their skin is a sickly gray color, and their eyes are like black pools. Their faces are expressionless, their arms hang loosely by their sides, and they simply stand there as if waiting for something. My limbs quiver with exhaustion but I keep my arm out protectively in front of me.

"Jane, what's wrong?" one of them questions in a tone filled with apprehension.

"Who the hell are you?! How do you know my name?" I shriek in a high-pitched and broken voice. I know how to defend myself, and I'll be damned if I let them hurt me without a fight.

"It's me," one of the monsters replies, taking a step closer.

In reaction, I quickly scurry sideways until my head slams against the cabinet and I reach up to clutch one of the vases tightly in my hand. "Don't come any closer!"

"It's Herb," he says with familiarity, but my mind is too foggy to comprehend. I'm overwhelmed with a sense of déjà vu, and my confusion intensifies as I try to remember how I ended up in this situation.

I take a step back, my voice trembling with fear. "Don't come any closer," I warn, but my strength is rapidly fading.

"Jane, please calm down," Herb pleads. "You're safe. There's no need to panic."

"STOP SAYING MY NAME!" I scream, my rage boiling over. My throat burns with pain, and I grasp at it, gasping for air.

As if on cue, the door bursts open, and a towering, humanoid monster strides into the room. I shrink back, my heart pounding in my chest as I take in his imposing figure. He gazes at me with intensity, his eyes drawing me in, and I can't help but feel a strange mix of fear and fascination.

I'm certain that this can't be real. Perhaps I'm still trapped in a nightmare, unable to wake up from this surreal scene.

A million questions race through my mind, but I'm too paralyzed by fear to form them into words. The monster's gaze is suffocating, crushing me under its weight, and I can feel my body shaking uncontrollably with cold sweat streaming down my face.

"Jane," he says. "You scared me. I thought I'd never see you again."

Then he opens his mouth to say something more, but I interrupt him with a sharp gesture. "Stop! Just stop talking. I can't handle this anymore. I need to get out of here." My voice quivers with anger and frustration.

I gasp for air, my chest heaving with the laborious effort of drawing breath. Hot air leaves my mouth as a loud whistle and my eyes cloud again until the monster is only a shadowy figure in front of me. A spark of rage ignites in my chest and I point right at him with a fiery accusation. He takes multiple steps back, confusion evident in his expression, but I barely notice it, lost as I am in the throes of a full-blown panic attack.

"You need to try to calm her down, Master Aldrick. She doesn't seem rational," the one called Herb says.

With a sigh, he shakes his head. "Maybe if I leave, you can talk her down the ledge," he says, and with that, he closes the door behind him with a dull thud as he leaves the room.

I want to run after him and demand to know why he is keeping me here, whoever the beast is. but

I can't seem to move. My body is aching and I feel so exhausted all of a sudden.

Herb cautiously approaches me. It's as if time has stopped and I have no will left to resist as he reaches out and places a trembling hand on my back. He moves it in slow circles as I take long, deep breaths, struggling to stay in control of the emotions raging through me.

"Who-who is that?" I whisper.

"That is Master Aldrick," Herb answers in a hushed tone. "He is the lord of this castle. But why do you ask? You already know him."

I scan the room quickly, taking in the peculiar decorations. I can just make out shadows whispering against the stone walls of what is a spacious bedroom in a castle.

It is hard for me to tell if these creatures are telling the truth, or if I have been lured into some kind of a cruel prank. I remember wanting to climb the mountain after Dorothy mentioned Sue. Apparently, Sue was kidnapped by a huge monster that resides on top of Mount Moorhead. She went around telling everyone that she was treated like a princess while out there. Also, she was apparently seduced by a giant creature and experienced the best sex of her life...

Oh no ... I am losing my ever-loving mind.

Herb steps back, his face contorting with concern. "I understand you're upset, Jane, but please, you must believe me when I say that you're safe here. Master Aldrick would never harm you."

I clench my fists at my sides, then Herb stops his soothing caress and lets his hand fall.

"I don't care about your words. I don't know you, I don't know him, and I don't know anything about what's going on here. All I know is that I want to leave this place and go back home."

Herb sighs, shaking his head. "I'm sorry, Jane, but that's not possible. Master Aldrick has brought you here for a reason, and he will not let you leave until he's ready."

My heart sinks. I'm trapped here, in this strange place with these monstrous creatures, and there's no way out. Tears well up in my eyes.

Herb seems to sense my distress and takes a step closer. "Jane, please try to calm down. I know this is all very overwhelming, but you need to stay strong. Master Aldrick is not your enemy. He wants to help you."

I am not in the mood to hear any more of his nonsense. "I don't believe you. I don't believe any of this."

His eyes turn so sad and my heart breaks a little, but I have no idea why. "Master Aldrick is not what you think he is. He's not a monster, not in the way you're imagining."

I stare at him, trying to make sense of what he's saying. A part of me wants to believe there's a reason why I'm here, but another part doesn't want to let go of my fear and mistrust.

"I need some time to think," I say finally, my voice barely above a whisper.

"Of course," Herb nods. "Take all the time you need. But please, try to keep an open mind. There's more to this than you realize."

With that, he turns, beckons to the other two to join him and starts to leave as I sink down on the bed, my head spinning. How did I end up here? And what is going to happen to me now?

"Wait!" I stop him before he opens the door. He turns to face me and takes a couple of steps toward me. "What kind of creatures are you?" I demand, my tone unintentionally harsh. Herb flashes a smile.

"We are an ancient race that once dominated these lands before the dawn of man. But now, we stick to the shadows and maintain our hold on whatever places we can in silence and seclusion," he answers calmly. "Knox and Teon are my brothers,

11

SOPHIA SMUT

and this is the world we know." He gestures to the
pair.

"Okay... But why am I here? What purpose do I
serve?" I hesitate, hoping for a familiar response that
never comes.

Herb's gaze falls to the floor as he considers his
words before speaking.

"You have been here before. You lived here for a
time and experienced things that you should not
have known about," he confesses solemnly. "Then
you came back. We notice you changed your hair
color, too. Very becoming."

I frown. "What on earth are you on about? If this
is some kind of sick joke, then end it right now!" I
exclaim in disbelief, ignoring his remark about my
hair. I can't recall changing the color at all. I pick up
one of the locks and play with it, staring at the deep
purple and teal hues. Meanwhile, I remind myself to
breathe, but the air doesn't seem to reach my lungs.
It all feels like a twisted joke.

"This isn't a game and there's no lying here. We
all know you." he declares, pointing to the two
motionless figures observing me, witnesses to my
internal struggle. I forgot they were even here. My
memories are fragmented, and I desperately want to
grasp at something familiar, but can't.

"You've been here before and you chose to stay with us. But when you left, something terrible happened. We weren't sure if you'd ever return. It's a miracle you're alive. You can thank us later for saving you from yourself. We believe your memory loss may have been caused by the accident."

"An accident?" I gasped, feeling overwhelmed by confusion and despair.

"It seems so," Knox replies, his voice breaking the oppressive silence that attends my shock. He carefully approaches us but stops when I flinch.

"You took a pretty bad fall and you hit your head," he explains. I raise a hand to my crown, now understanding why it's aching so much. Why all of me is aching. "That's why you can't remember anything right now."

I remain stunned, my gaze fixated on an endless abyss as I contemplate the harsh reality. Doubt creeps in, wriggling through my mind like a sieve, but I have no reason not to believe them. My stomach growls, startling me out of my thoughts. All three servants turn to me, and I see the crinkles at the corners of their eyes as they attempt to silently soothe me while I deal with my predicament.

"We'll get you something to eat and give you time to process all of this," Knox says at last. His words hang heavy in the air, and all three give me a nod before leaving me alone in the room. I'm overwhelmed with emotions, confusion, fear, and exhaustion topping the list.

My muscles are a mass of agony still, and I feel barely conscious. I fall back on the bed and sit still, too weary to contemplate or question anything. Suddenly, the door creaks open and two servants enter, carrying plates piled high with pancakes and glasses of juice. My stomach rumbles as I devour the food, not even considering where it came from. I'm starving, and the food tastes better than I expected.

As I eat, my energy slowly returns. I notice that the servants have left me alone again. Then, just like that, the giant monster Aldrick enters without so much as a knock, and my heart skips a beat. Fear and anticipation flood through me—what a strange mix of emotions. I have never seen a creature so massive. He's built like a mountain giant and has two large horns.

He stands by the door and his presence instantly fills the room like a thunderous storm. His piercing gaze cuts through my skin, attempting to unravel all my secrets. I try to resist but I am magnetically drawn to him, unable to pull away from his hold.

His voice is as cold and unwavering as a glacier

when he speaks, "Have they told you what happened?"

In response, I nod.

"So you know now that you are mine," he states with a conviction that sends chills down my spine ... followed by more confusion.

"Yours? What are you talking about?" I ask, about to lose it again.

Undeterred by my questions, Aldrick declares confidently, "You are mine. I am going to do all I can to make you remember all we have shared, and I will not let you leave until I achieve that."

His words echo like a distant drum, and there is no doubt in my mind that he means every single one.

CHAPTER
TWO

My heart nearly stops beating as Aldrick speaks to me. A chill of terror runs through my veins. I am a fortress of unanswered questions. What does he mean I am his? What does he mean he is going to make me remember all that we shared? And what does he mean he won't let me leave?

A burst of deranged laughter bubbles up my throat as I challenge him. "You cannot be serious, right?" I hope to keep an air of amusement so that maybe, just maybe, he will let me leave unharmed. But no, this man is not joking.

He stands twice my size and with one grip, he can break me into pieces. Deep down though, I have an unexplainable feeling that he won't hurt me. This thought is ridiculous because he is a monster, but despite that obvious fact, I am certain I am not in danger when he is around. There's no way I can outfight him and win, so all I have are my wits and persuasiveness. "This feels like a joke, like I am reliving my own nightmare," I tell him, sighing loudly.

"Do I look, to you, like a person who is likely to entertain the idea of a joke?" he asks, his tone and expression sharp and direct.

He seems the kind of monster that doesn't take any nonsense from anyone. I am paralyzed with fear as my heart pounds in my chest and a chill shoots up my spine. His voice is low and deep, radiating immense power like a feral beast. But there is something beautiful about the deepness of it, sounding like a forbidden lullaby, and I find myself getting pulled toward him.

His eyes glow like molten orange embers and a wave of heat radiates from his body, intoxicating me with his presence. His gaze is like a powerful vortex, sucking me in, and I struggle to look away for I am being dragged into the depths of an abyss. He is not content until our eyes lock again and he places his hand under my chin, lifting my head so that I am staring up into those strangely beautiful eyes once more.

What mysterious creature is he? A man? A beast? A god? What power does he hold over me?

"What are you doing?" I gasp as Aldrick towers over me.

"I am not doing anything to you," he growls, his deep voice vibrating within me. "You feel what your body is begging for. Our connection and bond are strong and real, and you can't fight this, no matter how hard you try."

The air between us crackles with electricity. With a force stronger than gravity, I am drawn toward him, drawn to the sweet and musky scent that hangs in the air, drawn to his eyes which glow like stars on his face, and drawn to the very essence of him which is nothing like I have felt before. He grips my chin in a possessive hold and my heart starts to race as my longing for him grows.

I want him to touch and consume me, to take in all of me and show me all of him. He must be telling the truth if I this strong emotion has captured me so wholly. There isn't any other explanation for how I feel. I can't believe I am experiencing such desire—this is wrong and insane. Beggars belief.

Suddenly, he steps back, shattering the spell

between us. His power over me is dizzying and it terrifies me. What am I doing having those kinds of thoughts about him? He's a monster.

"You need to let me go!" I blurt out hysterically. "My friends are waiting for me and there will be a rescue party. Someone will track me down all the way here."

He simply raises an eyebrow and says, "Dorothy?" With that single word, my body stiffens, my mind whirls.

"How do you know her name?" I choke out, staring at him in disbelief. This cannot be a coincidence.

"You'll find out soon enough," he replies mysteriously.

Another bitter laugh escapes my lips, a twisted kind of humor in the face of this darkness. "Every time I think I should trust you a little, you say something to make everything crumble again."

His gaze is steady and unyielding as he responds, "I haven't said anything outrageous. You belong to me."

A burning indignation that rises through my entire being. The nerve. "I. Do. Not. Belong. To. Anyone."

Aldrick's dark eyes drill into my very soul as if

he's trying to read my every thought. Long moments pass and I feel my skin growing hotter by the second until finally, he breaks the silence, his voice a low rumble like distant thunder, "All right then. My servants will come and make you presentable before we take a stroll around my garden—the one you've always loved so much. I like your new look, Jane, this new hair colour suits you."

Before I can so much as utter a reply, Aldrick spins on his heels and strides away, leaving me alone in the room with only my thoughts for company. Now that he is gone and his imposing presence is no longer bearing down upon me, I can finally allow my mind to wander back to where it all began: that horrible breakup with my ex, Sue's story, and my decision to climb Mount Moorhead.

But as I search through my memories, I find that a large gap has mysteriously appeared where I cannot recall what happened after I decided I was going to climb that blasted mountain, despite my friend Dorothy's warnings that this would be too dangerous and foolish.

I run my fingers through my hair and bring a lock closer to my face to examine it. Without a mirror, it appears that I may have gone a bit crazy with hair dye as my locks appear green ... and purple. I realize I need to see my reflection to determine if this was a good idea. I'm unsure if I should trust Aldrick and his servants, but I do believe my memories will return at some point. This experience seems like a dark fairy tale and I'm not ready to fully embrace it.

The three servants show up and escort me through a dark passage. The long walk fills me with trepidation. I analyze each door, curious about the secrets they may hold, but my attention is drawn to the sight of the servants' semi-erect cocks swaying between their legs with each step. Though I try to ignore the warmth in my stomach, my body betrays me. There is no way this is happening!

"You know this garden well," Knox says as he turns the knob of the door at the end of the hallway. "It has always been one of your favorite places in the castle."

My head jolts in disbelief as I fight the urge to deny what my senses tell me. I search my memory for proof but come up short. Right before I made the decision to climb the mountain, I had a normal life, albeit pretty dull with the occasional bump in the road. I yearned for adventure. They say to be careful what you wish for...

When the door opens and a sweet fragrance

wafts in, a spark ignites in my brain. Though I can't conjure any images, everything about the garden feels familiar.

It's absolutely gorgeous, colorful, and fresh with the most amazing landscaping. I have been here before, I am sure of it. The pathways, the flowers, the large bubbling pool beyond ... recognition buzzes within me at the sights.

Knox's voice breaks through my trance-like state.

"Do you remember any of it?" His piercing gaze bores into me as the others watch eagerly for my response.

"I think I remember some of it," I say hesitantly. How could this be? Was it a powerful spell of some sort? Maybe this was some silly trick cooked up by these three and their master. I can't help but feel a little like a child at a birthday party, overwhelmed by the mix of newness and familiarity of everything around me.

"How do I know this is not some ruse? A cruel joke?"

Herb recoils as I suggest the notion of Master Aldrick doing something "silly." "He does not use his powers for the purpose of seduction," he chastises in a cutting tone.

Teon mutters something beneath his breath, a whisper meant only for me to hear. "He can do that just by looking at you because you're his true mate."

My eyes widen and my skin prickles with shock. In the back of my mind, I'm equally amused and disturbed by the suggestion. I'm too scared to ask him about what he means by calling me his mate.

We reach the pool, and I don't even bother to check if it's safe to swim. All I see is the clean, sparkling water before me, beckoning me in. Without thought or hesitation, I begin to undress before the startled servants. My movements are almost automatic, as if my muscles are acting of their own accord.

When I'm completely naked, I step forward and dip a toe into the water, a test of assurance that soon becomes a full-body plunge into the depths. I have no idea why I decided to take all my clothes off. These creatures are staring at me with hunger in their eyes, and yet I don't feel ashamed. It's like I am used to being naked in front of them.

A shiver runs down my spine as Aldrick's commanding voice echoes through the garden. "Leave us," he says, appearing out of nowhere. I jerk my head in his direction and see him lounging like a lion on a bench, a tree to his right. I feel exposed, so I cross my arms over my chest in a gesture of modesty.

As commanded, the servants slowly retreat from the garden. I remain rooted to the spot, arms crossed, foot still half-submerged in the pool as Aldrick watches me from his perch like a god holding dominion over all of creation.

He is a beast, but I can't stop staring at his largely built chest and arms. I have never been with a man like that. My ex-boyfriend Brad was small compared to Aldrick, and there was just not enough physical attraction between us for me to enjoy sex. Brad was convinced of his prowess in the bedroom, but he never went beyond the conventional, and the tiny voice in my head tells me that Aldrick would probably give me the most sensual pleasure if I can get used to him.

I quickly shake off that thought before it gets implanted in my mind. This is still a monster I am looking at. One who is keeping me hostage in his castle.

"Do you plan to continue watching me?" I ask shakily, yet my tone holding a note of resolve.

Aldrick stands to his feet, enthralling me with his powerful form. His silky shirt and cotton pants are mere distractions, unable to hide the tight muscles that make tantalizing ripples across his body. I can't help but let my eyes wander as he strides past me, causing my heart to race in anticipation. When he stops and I finally look into his eyes, I see a reflection of my own desire burning back at me.

"Step into the pool," he commands in a voice that brooks no argument, and I find myself obeying without question. But when I look into his face one more time before taking my first step, for just a fleeting moment, I think I see a spark of something else—Hesitation? Vulnerability?—before it disappears, and Aldrick returns to the stoic being he always appears to be.

I hastily sink into the pool until the water covers me up to my neck. I am mesmerized by Aldrick's orange eyes which gleam with hidden power. When he strips off his shirt, revealing his perfect physique, my pulse quickens and my breath catches in my throat. I want him and can't deny it. The physical attraction between us is almost unbearable, and I sense he knows this, too.

Aldrick's smirk turns into a devious grin as he lowers his pants and then steps forward so he's barely covered in the glistening water. We keep our gazes locked in some sort of bizarre challenge while my stomach drops with anticipation of what may happen next.

My knees buckle beneath me, my mouth agape when I catch sight of his two giant cocks. Not one, but two. Speechless, I wonder if he used both of them on me before.

While acknowledging how wild the reality is, I swallow hard, imagining how would it feel to be penetrated by both at the same time. Heat envelopes my body, racing down between my legs and spreading at a feverish speed. This desperate need for closeness cannot be escaped.

The magnificent sight, shapes and sizes of his cocks make it impossible for me to even consider looking away. Meanwhile, Aldrick's playful smirk tells me he knows the effect he's having on me. I am so aroused and wet. The pleasure of watching him is too much to miss out on.

He takes a few steps toward me, only stopping when he towers over me in the pool. He is so close we can almost touch. His gaze is electric, captivating, and hypnotizing me as if I'm caught in a trance. I can no longer move and feel rooted to the spot, a fly stuck in a spider's web.

Aldrick grabs the bar of soap that sits poolside and now I see something new in his eyes. "I'm going to wash you, Jane," he informs me in a commanding tone.

I swallow hard and cannot manage so much as a nod.

He lathers the soap over my skin, leaving no part untouched. Electric currents pass between us. Then I feel a strange vibration in the water, like a thousand tiny bubbles surrounding my body as something takes me by surprise. It's Aldrick's two cocks, pulsing, alive, sending waves of pleasure around me that cause my skin to tingle and ignite with undeniable passion. I think I am seeing things because this can't be happening for real. His cocks cannot vibrate—right? Yet, my eyes tell me otherwise.

"What is happening?" I ask, looking right into his eyes.

"It means we are connected. It means I am close to my true mate and that I want to spill my seed inside you so you can bear my children," he growls, his tone low and raspy. His face becomes a rigid mask as though he's in pain. Then he pulls me to him and I become lost in his embrace. "You may not remember me, but this feeling remains the same. As you can see, I'm already hard for you."

He releases me and I stumble backward, missing his warmth already. His hands move to my shoulders and he turns me around to continue lathering me up from head to toe. I am not used to this kind of treatment. The warmth from his fingers ripples through my core. He is right, his two cocks are hard as rocks.

I never cared much about sex before, but the idea of intimacy with this monster fills me with excitement. His fingers barely brush my sensitive skin but each simple touch turns me so inside out, I fear that I might pass out. Every part of me trembles as he explores more and more of me until I can't take it anymore. I pull away and reach for a towel, murmuring a thank you that hangs in the air between us.

But before I can leave, he steps closer and grabs my chin as he did before with a firm grip, holding my gaze captive. "I will make you remember me, Jane," he says fiercely. "Until then, your body will ache so much that you won't be able to function ... but I won't touch you, not until you beg me for it."

THREE

When I query Herb about Aldrick's whereabouts, his vague answer sends a shiver of dread down my spine. I haven't laid eyes on my captor since he submerged me in the pool and although it has been only a few hours, it feels like days have gone by. His parting words reverberate in my mind and I've been having strange visions since then, which made it impossible to stop thinking about him. He is a complete stranger, but I desire him. We have this unexplained connection I can't explain.

From the garden, Aldrick lets me find my way back to the room without calling for assistance.

"You wouldn't leave me," he said with an eerie conviction that leaves me both captivated and uncomfortable at the same time. As I make my way to my room, my legs feel heavy, as if some invisible force is trying to hold me back from running away.

Once inside, the walls close in around me but not in an unpleasant way. It's a sort of comforting feeling, giving me the urge to stay here and solve this mystery. Every second I spend in this place, my curiosity grows ever stronger, pushing me to take action. Aldrick and his servants might be playing a cruel game on me, or they might be telling the truth. I need to find out what kind of past I have with these people and how deep this goes.

Herb sits across the room, peacefully reading a book that is almost as large as him. His presence only intensifies my need to follow my gut.

"I really need to see Aldrick again. Can you take me to him?" I ask firmly, my voice echoing in the silent room. Herb looks up from his oversized book, his pale face illuminated by a single lamp. The sheer intensity of his gaze ought to unnerve me, but I will not be deterred. I must know what kind of life I signed up for. I need to have all the answers.

"Master Aldrick does not enjoy people coming to him without being summoned," Herb warns, his right eyebrow arching with a silent warning.

"Yes, but if I'm truly his mate then that shouldn't

be an issue, right?" I counter. "I don't see why I can't see him. If we are supposed to be connected like that then I should be able to have access to him whenever I need to."

"I suppose so," he grudgingly acknowledges as he hops down from the chair. "But if he is in a temper when you meet him ... well, you'll bear the consequences. Sometimes he might be in one of his moods."

I swallow down my trepidation, giving Herb a careless shrug. "Fine. Let's go." I trail after him, my steps heavy as I wonder if I've made the wrong decision. Will I ever see the darker side of Master Aldrick?

The beast seems kind enough so far, but is his gentle behavior an act? After all, I am his captive and I am sure that just one glimpse of his true self will make my insides shake like a leaf. Yet, I'm not scared of him anymore. Maybe in the beginning, but not now.

"You must know," Herb says with an air of urgency, piercing my stupor with his words. "You went back to your world to sort out your affairs and then when you were coming back, you took a nasty fall. You hit your head so that's why you can't remember anything. At some point I am certain that these memories will come back to you. We are not trying to hide anything from you."

"I know all that," I say, then quickly add, "but I want answers and obviously Aldrick wouldn't have to hide anything from me."

"Yes," Herb replies with a hint of exasperation. "We can tell you what we know, but how much of it will you take as truth? How much of what I have told you so far do you believe?" He stops in front of a door, turning to me with an unwavering stare.

"Honestly? Not much," I admit. "It sounds totally implausible and I can't shake the thought that you're making this up. Still, I remember little things like the vases and the pool and somehow, I'm not sure anymore."

"Precisely," he intones. "Only your own memories will validate the situation and that is all we can hope for: that your memory comes back to life."

Herb stands like a sentinel in front of the imposing door. My palms break into a sweat as the door slowly swings open. When Herb strides in, his face looks like carved marble—expressionless and unyielding. But as he turns back, I swear I catch the flicker of a smirk on his face.

"Master Aldrick would like to see you," he says simply, standing aside.

My pulse thunders in my ears as I press my trembling hand against the door and push it further open. I feel like I'm stepping into another world as I cross the threshold into Aldrick's office. The air is thick with his presence and for an instant, I'm sure he can hear my heart hammering in my chest. He sits at his desk, a dark silhouette against a backdrop of parchment. It's difficult to judge if he is in a good or bad mood.

A large book lies open in front of him, and it feels like every secret hidden in its pages is casting its gaze on me. Perhaps we made love here in the past, I cannot help but wonder. But maybe it's not just me he wants, maybe I could be anyone—but I don't really believe that. Still, Aldrick seems like a beast that requires certain needs. I don't think he would be satisfied with just one quick fuck.

"I feel like I have been here before," I blurt out. He doesn't glance up from his book to acknowledge me, so I continue talking. "Watching you read from this side of the room."

Dread settles over me as he finally raises his gaze. "You are right. It isn't the first time," he says, his words echoing in my heart like a siren call. "It seems you have been missing me."

His words shock me and my cheeks flush with

heat. I try to find the mocking expression on his face that would indicate he is joking around, but all I see is softness. "I—I—" I stammer before he interrupts me.

"It's okay," he says, standing up and walking toward me. "You may not understand it yet, but our bond is so strong that even you can't ignore it."

I shake my head vehemently and open my mouth to object, but before I can say anything, he adds softly, "You are my mate and you will always seek me out."

"I have not been seeking you out," I argue, folding my arms over my chest. This 'man' is the most maddening creature I've ever met!

"So you won't argue being my mate. I guess that's a start," Aldrick states, clearly amused.

"I just need some answers to my questions," I reply, trying to keep my voice even. Aldrick needs to see that I have it together, even if I'm falling apart inside.

"Go ahead. Ask away," he answers, leaning back against the desk with a confident air.

"If it's true what everyone's telling me about you, how did you manage to seduce me?" I inquire, feeling a little silly that I am asking him such a question.

Aldrick tilts his head and mulls my words. "You make it seem like it was out of your control," he murmurs.

"Are you saying I chose to fall for you?"

The ensuing silence is almost too much to bear. All I can think of is surrendering to him, his hands exploring my body, pushing me down on the desk, and him pounding into me from behind with his two giant cocks.

"I'm saying there is nothing you have done that you did not freely choose," he says, his voice thick with meaning. Aldrick's eyes darken as he leans in closer. "But in a way, it wasn't entirely your choice, either. Our bond is nothing like you can fathom. You were drawn to me because we are meant to be together. It's fate. Destiny."

His words sink into my skin, resonating with something deep within me that I can't quite explain. But I refuse to believe in destiny, or any kind of supernatural force that runs my life. "I don't believe in fate. I think we make our own choices."

Aldrick's smirk fades, replaced by a serious expression. "You're right, to a certain extent," he concedes. "But there are forces beyond our control that shape our lives. You can't deny the chemistry between us, the way our bodies respond to each other. That's not something you can choose. It just is."

Oh, fuck.

The air crackles between us while I search for words that don't come.

What could I possibly say to him when I couldn't remember a thing about how this supposed bond started?

I swallow hard, conflicting emotions taking center stage. Part of me realizes this is madness, while another, despite fearing the unknown, wants to take this to wherever it leads. "I don't know if I'm ready ... for something like this, or if I ever will be," I admit at last, my voice barely above a whisper.

Aldrick reaches out and takes my hand. His touch singes my skin. "You don't have to torture yourself," he says in a gentle tone. "I'll be here when you are."

And for a moment, I allow myself to think I'm on to something worth exploring...

"How on Earth did I end up here?" I inch closer to him, closing the distance between us. "I remember leaving my home, coming to Mount Moorhead, then hiking up the paths. That's it."

"Well," Aldrick declares. "It was purely by chance that you stumbled upon this castle and I let you in. We felt an instant connection and eventually, it became undeniable. We couldn't resist any longer and we … made love multiple times. You agreed to bear me children and I thought you'd never return to living in the human world…"

A lump forms in my throat and I shift awkwardly on my feet. He cannot be serious. I agreed to give him children—as in not one, but multiple? This sounds like a crazy thing to expect, especially in the twenty-first century.

But this monster clearly lived in some other time, as well as dimension. It seems that for him, such a situation is normal. Personally, I don't think I am ready to become a mother.

Judging from his wicked smile, Aldrick must see how much his words affect me. In a short time, I picked up on his penchant for shocking me with some brutish statement, weaved into a core of kindness. Just now, I refuse to give him the satisfaction of seeing me squirm, so I stand to my full height. "Go on with the story," I say with a forced level of confidence.

"After a while, I could tell you missed your world even though you never said anything. You had people there who would be concerned about you. You must have understood that time in this castle passes much slower than in the outside world, so you could stay here for a long while and your friends would barely notice."

My ears perk up and my eyes widen, completely taken aback by this news. "I don't believe that is possible. I have many friends and they would worry about me." I say.

Aldrick shrugs. "Does it make you happy that you can stay here for as long as you like?"

I roll my eyes in response. "I don't care about that. So, back to what you were saying, I got injured in a fall on my way back?"

He nods. "That's right. We're in this odd spot now where we have to start over again."

In his gaze, I find no hint of deceit. Since I awoke to the sound of Aldrick and his servants telling me their version of events, I have only sought out signs that can suggest otherwise and bring their house of lies to the ground. But now, as I face him, I know he's chipping away at my doubts, one word, one gaze at a time.

"It must be hard for you then," I say.

"What do you mean?" he asks, looking slightly confused.

"If we made that kind of deep connection then it must be really difficult for you to see me like this, unable to remember you or any of the good moments we might have shared..."

Aldrick sits in silence for what feels like an eternity. Just as I'm wondering if I've gone too far, he stands and advances toward me. I'm uncertain if I've made a misstep or how I should react. Before I can decide, he's standing right before me. In my peripheral vision, I notice his arm raised and instinctively close my eyes, preparing for a punch. My breath catches in my throat and I purse my lips, but no blow comes. Instead, I feel his gentle hand on my cheek and his lips pressed against my forehead.

As I slowly open my eyes, I meet Aldrick's gaze, so full of love. My worries and concerns vanish like a wisp of air and my body relaxes. Aldrick seems to sense this as his hand finds its way to the small of my back and provides me comfort.

"You have no idea," he says, his voice laced with raw sensuality. "I wish I could make you remember all we shared because we had something so special. Something I never thought I'd find."

I don't know if I moved or he moved or we both moved but before anyone of us could say another word, the short distance between us has closed and our lips are pressed together. Kissing Aldrick is nothing like I could recall experiencing. Although the action is all on my lips, the sensation of it affects my entire body. Every inch from the top of my head to the tip of my toes, Aldrick's touch rages through me like an inferno. Because of his height, I have to stand on my tiptoes and he has to lean down but our lips dance effortlessly despite our uncomfortable positions. With the hand he has on my back, Aldrick pulls me closer to him. I gasp into his mouth when my breasts bump into his chest, pressing myself further into him because I cannot have enough.

Instinctively, I wrap my arms around him. While Aldrick's one hand is enough to hold my entire body, mine are only able to hold onto small parts of him. My right hand is stretched to the limit to rest on the nape of his neck while the left grabs onto his arm for dear life. The more we kiss, the more electric and passionate it gets. He is slowly devouring my mouth and I let go of a desperate moan, wanting and needing more.

I rub along his arms and feel the hardness of his chest and abs. He trails his hand from my cheek to my hair, ruffling it up and massaging my scalp. In a rough but painless motion, he tilts my head backward and sideways, breaking our kiss.

I'm breathless and my lips are swollen. I do not even get a look at his face before he buries it in the exposed skin of my neck. A moan escapes my lips once again and my eyes gloss over as he sucks on my skin.

Aldrick is the only thing keeping me standing for I am too dizzy with bliss to rely on my feet. I can barely process what I'm feeling as his hands roam my body and his exploring mouth sends my mind into a tailspin. He brushes his lips along my neck, nipping the sensitive skin there. My hand is in his hair as he continues to travel down to my chest, leaving a trail of kisses, teasing and tickling me with his tongue. I'm aching for him in a way I never ached for Brad or anyone else.

As he settles his face upon my breasts, his horns flank my head on both sides so I am wrapped in the cocoon of his body all over. There is nowhere else I'd be. I rub whatever bit of him I can reach while he draws patterns over my skin with his large hand.

I trail my fingers over his chest, down past his abs to his groin, then reach out with my other hand to grab his tail. A deep growl escapes his mouth as I push my hand against his cock through his clothes. In response, his hand finds its way between my thighs and I bite my lips hard as he starts to stroke my sex. My pussy pulsates with every stroke of his fingers and my hips buck, seeking more of that sensual touch.

The reality of the situation hits me like a wave and I become aware of how powerless I am at this moment. Even though my body begs for more, I'm not sure this is something I should be doing. How could I be submitting to this creature's desires simply because his words are convincing? How far am I even willing to take this?

"Aldrick..." My voice comes out unexpectedly seductive. "Aldrick, we have to stop."

He lifts his head from my cleavage but does not release me from his embrace, for which I am quietly grateful. His eyes dim and our labored breathing eases.

"I don't think this is such a good idea," I suggest.

If he is disappointed, he does not show it. He slowly pulls away and I instantly want to yank his hands back to my skin. He must know that I have temporarily lost the ability to stand upright because he continues to hold me by the waist until he is certain that my knees are not going to buckle so I'll fall flat on my face.

"I could not resist," he murmurs. "You're mine, Jane, and you know this. Your body begged me to touch you."

I want to tell him that I do not require any explanation from him and that I know what I'm feeling, but before I can open my mouth to respond, an orb placed in the corner of the room behind him starts to glow and completely diverts my attention.

"What is that?" I ask, pointing at the object.

Aldrick turns around, grunts then rushes to it. Something has shifted and whatever moment we might have just shared has passed. Aldrick stands next to the orb and examines it without touching it as if worried that something might jump out of it.

"Aldrick, is everything okay?" I ask, even though I doubt he'll respond.

"No," he says with a dry chuckle, surprising me. "Looks like we are about to have company."

CHAPTER
FOUR

"Unexpected guest?" I press. Aldrick ignores me, rushing around the room as though the idea of having a company is a bad thing. I stand there confused as he gathers books, reinforces locks and looks quite disturbed. "Aldrick! Talk to me!" With that I grab his attention, and he stops in his tracks, facing me with a troubled expression.

I expect him to say something, yet instead he calls out for Herb.

"I'm not going anywhere until you explain to me what's going on," I say. "I don't want to be stuck in my room again."

"I will tell you everything later. Now just go with

Herb and wait for me while I deal with this situation," he says and before I can ask about anything else, Herb saunters into the room and narrows his eyes at the glowing orb. His face reveals that he needs no explanation for what is about to happen next. *He* knows.

"Please accompany Jane to her room and make sure she stays there," Aldrick snaps, not deigning me with so much as a glance.

"So I'm back to being a prisoner again?" I hiss through clenched teeth, my fury bubbling like a boiling cauldron. He cannot be serious and I am not planning to move, so I fold my arms over my chest and glare at him.

"It is for your own safety. You have to trust me, Jane," he replies noncommittally. Still, his eyes never meet mine.

Herb strides up to me and throws open the door, offering me no choice but to walk through it. With a huff, I follow the servant while Aldrick shuffles through a book before furtively tucking something into his pocket—a scrap of paper that screams of secrets and unanswered questions. I came here expecting answers but now I am more confused than ever. And frankly, this is starting to annoying me. I feel like I have no say in anything that is going on in this castle.

I scurry after Herb down the hallway, desperate to understand the mysterious danger that has supposedly crept into our castle. His silence speaks volumes and yet I force the question out of my lips, "Herb, who is this guest?

He turns to me with a stern expression, annoyed by my persistence. "I am not at liberty to tell you that."

I exhale sharply, telling myself to stay calm. "If this castle is going to be under some sort of threat, should I not be made aware of it? If anything happens to you or Aldrick, then I am not safe, either!"

Herb's mouth curves downward as he stops in front of my door and unlocks it. His voice is barely above a whisper as he speaks with finality, "If this castle were truly in danger, then it would be better for everyone if you stayed out of the way."

Then he slams the door in my face and my mind is instantly flooded with memories. Suddenly I feel lightheaded and the room spins around me. Like the other fragmented memories I've been trying to piece together, these appear in flashes. In the scene playing in my head, I'm in the pool, stark naked.

Herb is there as well as Teon and Knox. Herb is pushing his big cock into me, pounding me against the edge of the pool while Teon and Knox watch and pleasure themselves. These memories are so vivid and so erotic.

I shake my head in an attempt to dispel the vision that lingers with me as I start pacing around my room, telling myself not to get distracted. There is no way any of that can be true unless I am going insane. Besides, this is not the right time to engage in a battle with my own brain.

I walk away from the door and try to find my balance by resting against the wall. Just then, I remember Sue and her stories, which do not seem so bogus now. Sue did say something about a monster but she also mentioned his servants, I believe. Did I also experience all that? I feel myself get wet at that thought alone, excitement taking over my initial confusion.

Again, not the right time, but what can I do now, trapped as I am within these four walls?

In my loneliness, my fear and agitation intensify. Is Aldrick in the midst of danger and what can I do to help? I keep on pacing, my thoughts spinning faster than my feet as I frantically seek an answer that doesn't seem to exist. They are not coming back for me. I start pounding on the door, desperately hoping Herb is still on the other side and that he finds it in his heart to answer me. But when no response comes, I collapse on the bed and bury my face in the sheets.

All the emotions of the past hour finally take me under. Touching Aldrick and being touched by him, kissing him, and then being hurried out in that manner ... then flashbacks of moments with Herb, Knox, and Teon. I want to cry and scream and break something, let my frustrations free through an outward violent expression. But I do not do any of that. I simply stay still and close my eyes.

My eyes open to find Herb, Teon, and Knox standing in front of me, their large erect cocks preceding them. Lost as I was in my turmoil, I did not hear them come in. But that is not the only weird thing. When I look around, I realize that we are no longer in my room. We are beside the pool and although the scene seems like they are just about to give me an impromptu bath, their eyes suggest some deeper—a more animalistic intent.

I am dreaming again. This is not happening for real, so I must have fallen asleep...

"Let us begin," I say for I sense they are waiting

for my permission. After all it's my dream, so I should be the one directing it.

Herb grabs his cock and starts to gently stroke it while Teon and Knox walk over to me and proceed to remove my clothes. I do not protest. In fact, I enjoy how they tear the garments off me and toss the shreds on the ground.

I stand naked in the pool as the servants approach, each armed with soaps and sponges. "Herb, take care of my chest," I demand. "Teon and Knox, focus on my legs and feet." They obey without hesitation, and I feel important.

Herb caresses my breasts tenderly, tracing circles around the sensitive areas until my body shudders. Teon and Knox massage my thighs but spend most of their time between my legs, lightly touching and teasing me with the promise of something more, fingers trailing my entrance but never truly going in. I like being the one in control, being taken care of.

Just as I start to feel great pleasure, Aldrick's voice brings me back to reality and I see him standing beside the pool. "Leave us," he says, and the servants immediately stop, get out of the pool, then disappear from the garden.

His forceful manner is both thrilling and intimidating. He unzips his pants and one of his enormous

SOPHIA SMUT

cocks springs out. A gasp escapes my lips as I recall his intentions—he wants to fuck me and conceive a child, I am certain of it.

That thought terrifies me so I quickly exit the pool and make an escape, naked. Aldrick shouts after me but I am too scared to listen. I can hear him about to catch up with me, but I don't let that stop me from getting as far away from him as possible. I take off down the dark hallway, pushing through the door at the end of it until I'm in a pitch-black forest. I can hardly make out where I'm going, yet I keep running. Eventually, I end up in a cave that's as quiet as a graveyard and duck behind a rock, hoping I managed to outrun Aldrick.

Aldrick's voice rumbles from behind me, sending a chill down my back. "Can you really hide from me?" he questions.

I let out a terrified yell as he roughly spins me around and shoves me face-first against the cave wall.

"You belong to me," he whispers as I feel both of his shafts nudging my entrance from behind. I cry out as he thrusts one of his giant cocks into me. I'm not ready and he is huge.

I let out a sound that is part agony, part ecstasy

as Aldrick pulls my hair and thrusts his larger cock into me, moving hard and fast.

"You thought you could escape me, but I always find you," he growls, making me lose my mind.

I moan loudly, wanting more of him, but he lets go of me and I open my eyes.

I'm back in my room, fully awake. I have been dreaming. A moment later the door swings open and I pull the sheet instinctively to my chest. Knox is standing in the doorway with a smug smirk playing on his lips. In his hands are folded articles of clothing and peaceful normalcy reigns all around.

"What is it?" I gasp, getting back to my feet.

"Master Aldrick wants you to have dinner with him and his guests," Knox answers casually before placing the clothes on the bed. His voice carries a sinister undercurrent that makes me shudder.

"Guests?" I ask, my fear making the word come out in a shrill screech. "Who are they?"

Knox takes a long pause before answering, "I believe Master Aldrick would rather do the introductions himself." His gaze burns into me before he makes to depart.

"Wait!" I say sharply, desperation lacing my words. Knox stops and slowly looks over his shoulder at me. "There has to be something you can

tell me ... something that can prepare me for what I
am about to step into."

Knox hesitates again, then says, "Very well." He
pauses, releasing a huff of breath. "You just have to
be the most glamorous version of yourself. Master
Aldrick's guests love beauty. We will return to get
you in twenty minutes, so get ready."

"What?" His 'hint' only serves to puzzle me
further. But Knox offers no additional reply and I
roar in frustration. He vanishes before I can probe
more, shutting the door behind him. What is wrong
with these servants? They stroll in, give me orders,
then leave. Totally unacceptable.

As my gaze shifts from the door to the dresses
laid out on the bed, my temples throb with a pain so
intense, it knocks the wind out of me. Holding my
head in my hands, I squeeze my eyes shut, desperately trying to recall what my brain is so determined
to make me remember. More vivid images fill my
mind and I remember each of the times I change
into one of these princess-like dresses that seem to
possess a mysterious power. I can almost feel the
soft fabric on my skin as I slip into them, yet no
matter how hard I try, I cannot make out what
happens afterward.

My heart races in anticipation as I hurriedly slip

out of the old dress and into the new one. I stand before the mirror and take it in, a light blue masterpiece with a simple yet elegant design that draws attention to the wearer. The fabric fits me like a glove, molding around every curve and dip of my body. My breasts perk up, supported beautifully, and my waist appears narrower than it ever has, even before I've tightened the laces in the back. I'm taken aback at how incredible I look, my heart pounding its approval. With minutes to spare before the event, I tackle my hair with vigor, until not a single strand is out of place in a sleek and tight bun.

When Herb, Knox, and Teon return, I am ready, except my dress is still unfastened. For a moment, they are stunned into silence, their eyes transfixed on my silhouette. I break the hush with one question; "I need my dress fastened."

"Master Aldrick always does that for you," Teon responds.

At that moment, images of Aldrick's cold breath against my neck and his fingers pulling at my clothes flood my mind and I get dizzy again. I grab onto the wall for support. The silence is heavy, riddled with a sense of anticipation as I grapple with my mess of nerves.

"Are you okay?" Herb asks, taking a step forward toward me.

I clear my throat and place a hand on my forehead before opening my eyes. "I'm fine," I say. "I just remembered something."

"That is fantastic," Knox says with a smile. "May I ask what?"

"It's nothing big. Just short moments where Aldrick helped me fasten my dress."

"Do you think you remembered because of what Teon said?" Herb asks.

"Yes," I reply with a nod. "It is not the first time that has happened. Sometimes, when somebody mentions something I ought to remember or does something similar, I get those flashes."

"Your memory is returning," Herb says. "That is great news."

"Is it?" I find myself unable to hide the skepticism I am feeling. "They are barely memories. Just short bits of what ought to be extended parts of days I ought to remember."

"Oh, Jane." Teon smiles. "We should not try to rush your healing. Give your brain the space to regain its abilities on its own. Besides, memories do not work in the way you described. I mean, how many days can you truly remember in full? Once they pass, you only recall the significant bits and after a while, you even begin to muddle them up."

"I suppose you are right," I say with a sigh. "I just need everything to make sense."

"And it will," Herb says. "We promise you that."

Knox forces a smile as he and Herb lead me toward an unknown fate. When we arrive, the cacophony of voices beyond the door grow louder and more aggressive. Aldrick's deep booming voice rises above the rest, a force of destruction that could bring down any structure not fortified by stone.

"Should we go in?" I whisper, stopping myself from begging Herb not to open the door.

The sound of shattering glass and wild shrieking continues to increase.

"You wanted to know who Master Aldrick's guests are. Now you get to do that," he says before pushing the door open. The scene that awaits us is one of pure chaos.

But then, everybody freezes, their attention diverted to me.

I step into a fresh silence that suddenly engulfs the dining hall, as if a raging fire has been extinguished and only smoldering ashes remain. Standing in the doorway, I shift from one foot to the other, my eyes wide as I take in the scene before me.

Anxiety swells in my chest until I finally lock onto a figure across the room—Aldrick. His presence is like a beacon, and I can feel his intensity from where I stand.

Why am I so nervous though? This is just dinner and Aldrick is a monster. I don't know anybody here and clearly, Aldrick deems it safe enough for me to join in the activities. I don't need to prove anything to anyone.

Yet as the entire table of guests sizes me up, as if waiting for something to happen, I have never felt so intimidated in my life.

Aldrick sits at the head of the table, displaying a calm exterior. But beneath his mask is a menacing presence, and his stare is laden with warmth and desire. I am not wrong, I can see it in his eyes. To his left is an almost identical man, also horned but with lighter, platinum blond hair and a wicked smirk. To his right sit two women of his species, not as tall and with horns far more curved, giving off a more graceful air. Their faces are so fair, I fear I might see through them, and the redness of their lips makes for a sharp contrast against their skin. One wears a yellow dress and smiles at me gently, while the other dons a red dress and sports the exact same wicked expression as her companion.

"Jane, everybody is waiting for you," Herb whispers to me, snapping me out of my mini-trance.

Aldrick's eyes are piercing through me like a thousand needles jabbing into my skin, rousing me from my stupor.

"Right," I say and then step forward. The clanking of my shoes ricochets off the walls like a thousand hammers, assaulting my senses. I try to move faster, desperate to outrun the clanking, but the sound only intensifies, piercing my ears and leaving me helpless in front of my dumbfounded audience.

The haphazard ringing continues, echoing through the room, reverberating in my skull as Aldrick stands off to the side, seemingly unaware of my humiliation.

"Nice shoes," the lady in red dress says, her tone dripping with sarcasm. She arches a brow, then winks.

"Shut it, Khimaira," the lady in yellow says before flashing me a soothing smile that is not sufficient to calm my nerves. "I'm Lena. It's nice to finally meet you, Jane."

"N-nice to meet you too," I manage to blurt out before stopping in front of Aldrick. "I need your help".

Aldrick springs to his feet in response to my words and goes behind me, his action a fierce declaration of ownership to the guests. The heat radiating from his body melts away the gap between us until I am completely and utterly possessed. His fingertips ignite a trail of fire as they stroke my neck. All noise fades away until all I am aware of is Aldrick, and I close my eyes in surrender to his touch. My skin is almost hums with his energy and scent that surrounds me.

Suddenly, a deep voice cuts through the fog, pulling me back to reality. I tell myself to keep breathing.

"Isn't that beautiful?" My eyes snap open to see the male guest watching us, question punctuated with a sarcastic lilt that speaks volumes.

"Don't start, Karken," Lena warns.

"What? It's not as if her kind did not almost ruin our family," Karken retorts, and the woman next to him chokes on her drink as she tries to stifle laughter.

Aldrick tightens my dress so much, I can barely breathe. His lips curl into a crooked smile as he draws out the chair next to Lena, silently beckoning me to follow. He then returns to his seat at the head of the table and I hesitantly make my way over to my chair, carefully avoiding Karken's menacing glare.

"Isn't it too early to be asking for punishment?" Aldrick speaks calmly, his face a mask of amusement, but his words are laced with a clear warning.

Karken briefly sets his mean gaze on me before focusing on his glass of wine and I know then that I should watch my back.

"My apologies, Jane. This is my brother, Karken, and his mate, Khimaira. And this is my sister, Lena."

"Nice to meet you all," I say in a polite tone, but when I meet their eyes I can tell that something sinister lurks beneath the surface. Intimidated by their intensity, I lower my gaze and silently prepare for an uphill battle. It seems that this is going to be a long drawn out dinner indeed.

"So, tell me," Lena says, breaking the silence. "Have you been told of all the traditions required of Aldrick's mate?"

"Lena..." Aldrick cautions.

"If this woman is your mate, surely she must know these things," Lena says, undeterred by Aldrick's tone. "She needs to be prepared."

"I'm not so certain that I am Aldrick's mate," I interject.

"Oh." An expression flashes through her face, too

quick for me to understand. "That is all right then. You should not worry about potions or whatever."

"Jane is my mate, Lena, so quit it," Aldrick says emphatically.

"Trouble in paradise," Karken whispers cynically under his breath.

"Well, I guess we will see how things turn out." Lena takes a sip of her drink. When she drops her glass, our eyes meet and she smiles at me. For once, I actually think I might be able to make a friend here.

CHAPTER
FIVE

"W hat are you reading?" Karken asks from behind me, startling me. I spin around in surprise, dropping my book in my lap. I was attempting to lose myself in its pages, but Karken and Khimaira disturb that process by showing up in the garden completely out of the blue. I arrived here with Aldrick, but he left with one of his servants, promising to be back soon.

I am annoyed that Aldrick vanished and now I have to deal with his siblings on my own. Maybe he did it deliberately as some sort of test to see if I'm worthy of being his mate.

Then I remember what he said after dinner that went on for hours last night. The servants kept bringing food and Aldrick entertained his guests with my presence. So I fixed a smile on my face, trying to get involved in the conversation, but it seemed Lena had a lot to say on almost every subject and I only managed to get through the dinner by drinking that delicious wine Herb kept pouring for me. Aldrick's sister surely likes the sound of her own voice.

When it was over, Aldrick took me back to my room. Before he let me go to sleep, he smiled at me, brushed his finger over my cheek, and said, "Be warned—my siblings are not to be trusted. If I had my way, you'd never have to deal with them. But somehow, they got wind of your presence here and demanded to meet you. It's almost as if they were drawn to you, so be careful."

The rumble of his voice was like an earthquake that shook my very foundation. His words were a hammer striking the anvil of my soul, each syllable echoing with the promise of certain doom. I was held captive in the grip of his power, unable to look away as his words of caution lingered in the air.

"I will take care of myself, Aldrick. I don't think I need your help, thank you very much," I seethed, my words dripping with molten anger. I was ready to tell him that rather than warning me, he should have given me more detailed explanation *before* dinner. I was angry with how things turned out last night. He shouldn't have locked me in my room in the first place.

"No, you won't manage it alone," he jeered, his hoarse laughter echoing through the room. "Not against them."

Then today he came to my room in the morning, telling me that he was eager to show me something in his study. I was still annoyed and apprehensive about everything that happened, but I was willing to pretend that eventually, he would chose to share more things. Aldrick handed me a book he wanted me to read. His eyes bore deep into me and his voice carried an unspoken demand. "I need to hear your thoughts about this", he said before striding away into the garden, leaving me to follow in his wake.

Aldrick's deep baritone voice filled the air with enchantment as he described his intricate family tree, page after page, revealing the faces and names that wove together like a complex tapestry. I got lost in its intricacies but his voice was the beacon that brought me back, captivated by its soothing melody as my mind pondered the revelations.

At some point, I pretended to be confused just so I could hear him go through the family tree again. But before I could process exactly what he was reading to me, Herb suddenly appeared, demanding Aldrick's attention for a pressing matter. My chest tightened as I watched them walk away, leaving me behind with questions of why I felt so disappointed in the first place.

Karken and Khimaira now tower over me, their eyes narrowing and brows furrowing with suspicious curiosity. Their glares feel like a cloud pressing against me from all sides. I hope that Aldrick won't be long because I don't want to be alone with the two of them. I now agree with him that I shouldn't trust them.

"It's just a little history book," I say, hoping they would take the hint and leave me alone. Karken ignores me, settling onto the couch to my right with a thud while Khimaira perches on the arm of the couch on my left. They surround me in a triangle of tension, trapping me in the center like a fly in a spider's web. I squirm uncomfortably, only managing to make things worse as I'm unable to free myself from their watchful gazes.

"I would just like to read this book in peace," I say, trying one last time. "Aldrick will return in a minute or two."

Karken's mouth twitches into a smirk as he tilts his head to meet my gaze. His piercing green eyes are like those of a wild animal, and I feel like I've been ensnared in their depths. I don't know what to make of his character—he isn't like Aldrick, that I can see, but the truth is that I don't know him at all. This whole world is foreign to me.

"Do you trust Aldrick?" he asks unnervingly.

I respond with a meek, "I suppose I do."

His magnetism radiates from him in every direction, and it is obvious that Karken and Aldrick share the same kind of power, but while Aldrick's presence is inviting, Karken's comes off as sinister and oppressive. He leaves an imprint that draws people in and holds them in a vise as they are unable to escape his mysterious allure.

"It's actually better for him if you don't get your memories back." He chuckles.

"What exactly do you mean by that?" I ask warily.

"The less you remember, the more easily he can twist your memories and create an alternate version of reality to benefit himself," he informs me with a dismissive wave of his hand.

The garden air crackles with palpable tension as Karken steps closer, his powerful aura much like a physical force pressing against me. Every fiber of my being begs to stand and face him, but I remain rooted in place, glued to the seat. Out of the corner of my eye, I spot Khimaira observing me, her lips curling into a satisfied smirk. Her cryptic messages require more thought than Karken's straightforward words, and have a greater impact on me than I could ever explain. Khimaira's covert tactics are the true weapons in her arsenal, and no matter how hard I try, they remain unreadable.

"Good thing he's not the only one here in this cursed castle," Karken seethes, jumping up and snatching my attention away from Khimaira's face. "That would be even worse."

"Knox, Herb, and Teon live here, too," I reluctantly stammer out.

Karken releases a mocking laugh that quickly fades away into an awkward silence that stretches for a long moment. "They're nothing but Aldrick's mindless puppets. No more than the extensions he uses to speak his thoughts and do his bidding."

He glides back to the chair and places his right hand menacingly on my thigh as he sits while his left hand rests on the nape of my neck, squeezing it gently. His touch feels like a live-wire sparking with electricity, teetering on the edge between pleasure and peril. He seems comfortable with me, a little too comfortable. I haven't been here long, but I am certain that Aldrick won't be happy once he sees him touching me. I am ready to yank his hand off me, but I choose to wait.

"Apart from the servants there isn't anyone else here, right?" I say, my voice echoing. "Who else in this castle can help me?"

A triumphant smirk forms on Karken's lips. It is as smug as it is beautiful. "Me," he declares. "Come to me."

"But you just arrived here and I don't know you. How could you know anything about what has happened here?"

"No, Jane," he says, his voice resonating like thunder. "You are the only one who just arrived here. I've known my brother since I was a child and I can expose whatever lies he has been feeding you before it's too late." His eyes burn with ferocity and his jaw is set with grim determination.

"Aldrick is lying to me?" I ask in disbelief. "Why?"

Karken's smirk turns into a victorious grin. "A lord with no mate will do whatever it takes to fill the void in his miserable life."

Before I see Aldrick approaching, my skin ripples with heat as his powerful presence washes over me, making Karken's words and warnings vanish in an instant. Aldrick's voice shakes the walls as he snarls, rage flaring from his very pores like a raging inferno.

"What are you doing here, Karken?"

"Brother," Karken says, a smug grin crawling up his face, but he doesn't move his hand off my thigh, which is surprising. "Jane and I are having a light conversation. We were just talking about you and you have nothing to concern yourself with."

"Leave us be," Aldrick demands coldly. "Jane and I are in the midst of something."

"As you wish, brother," Karken responds quietly, an eerie stillness settling over him as he raises one hand in a mock gesture of defeat. "It is your castle. C'mon Khimaira, let's leave them to ignite their passion."

"Goodbye, Jane." Khimaira's icy tone cuts through the air like a blade as she stands. With a swift, almost deliberate movement of her wrists, her fingers trace the necklace around my neck and the back of her hand harshly brushes my cheek. The piercing touch almost burns my skin and I cannot repress the dread that lingers in my heart. Karken and Khimaira walk away, holding each other's hands and giggling like a couple of teenagers. There is obviously a bond between them and I feel a little envious of them, for some reason.

"Is that what you want us to be?" I ask as Aldrick sits beside me. His face has now softened into a vision of calm and tenderness.

"What do you mean?" he replies, his voice gentle and reassuring.

"Do you want us to be like Karken and Khimaira?" My body tenses as anger rears its head. "Is that why you keep insisting on us being mates?"

Aldrick's lips curl into a sinister smirk, eyes narrowing to slits as he gazes at the fountain ahead. "Karken and Khimaira are not the best role models for us, Jane." His voice is thick with emotion. "There is no need to compare our relationship to theirs. What we have is entirely different—it's something that has been broken and must be mended."

"They seem happy," I pipe up softly.

Aldrick's deep gaze returns to me and I can feel the intensity radiating from him as he speaks, "You are my mate simply because you were always destined for me. There needs to be no comparison between us and them."

His eyes narrow at the corners.

"If only they could pretend themselves into contentment as they have done with happiness," he says as he rises from his chair. He walks over to the fountain and sits on its edge, directly facing me. His face softens and the world around us seems to fade away. The soft sound of the water pouring from the fountain is all I can hear as he asks, "How long did they sit with you for?"

"Just a few minutes," I say, my voice hesitant and thin.

"I know my brother," he says. "He can spew out enough words to fill an encyclopedia in that short amount of time."

I can't help but chuckle a little, the sound thick with disbelief. "It seems he has a lot to say."

Aldrick's expression shifts, the smile vanishing. "Do not take everything he says too seriously, my dear Jane. He loves to provoke, and the only time he gets satisfaction is when you give in to his games. Do not let him cloud your judgment. My brother is often bored, so he will keep pushing your buttons until you spill all your secrets to him."

Aldrick's words sink into my skin like a noxious fog, a reminder of the awkwardness that resonates between these two brothers. I can almost taste the distrust as it permeates the air around us, and an unwelcome pressure takes hold for me to choose one side or the other. But my curiosity is too great and I resist, instead focusing on my own questions.

"That's enough about Karken and Khimaira,"

Aldrick snaps, as if he can see the subject makes me uncomfortable. "They are the least of our worries. Tell me what you have read from that book."

His gaze sends a shiver down my spine for it feels like he is trying to unravel me, slowly and deliberately. No matter how hard I try, I cannot build a wall high and thick enough to keep out the attraction between us.

"*The Tribes of the Old Mountains* is a misnomer and an outright lie," I proclaim loudly. His expression remains stoic, but I can see the amusement in his eyes. "This book is not about all the tribes, only your own family and their history, and barely even mentions the others," I continue, my voice rising as I fight to keep control of my emotions. "History should be told truthfully, not just to flatter your royal family."

"Hmm." Aldrick's eyes are like two deep wells, their darkness drawing me in with a power I have never known before. My gaze is fixed on him like a magnet, my fingers tingling with anticipation to explore the muscular planes of his body. His clothes barely contain the strength that radiates from him, and when he speaks my mind is muddled by the sudden heat that envelopes my body. "I'll be sure to remember this moment when I'm writing the next volume," he murmurs.

My heart skips as disbelief hits me. Aldrick is laughing at me, pounding the book he is holding in his hand before reaching out to me with it. I take it with trembling hands and flip over to the front, looking for the author's name, only to find the hard binding completely blank. Inside the book is a short note and underneath it, Aldrick's name is scrawled in exquisite penmanship. I am so embarrassed and find myself speechless.

Aldrick looks like he has won a coveted prize but then waves me off as if asking me to stop being embarrassed. His actions of kindness catch me off guard and all I can do is be amazed at this creature that is far more decent than any human man I have ever met.

"It's just something I wrote when I was younger. Maybe in a short while from now, I will write something more interesting," he says with a mischievous glint in his eyes that fills me with excitement. "A muse is a hard treasure to find these days."

I stumble toward the fountain to stand beside Aldrick. Gripping the edge of the pool with both hands, I try to haul myself up but then a sharp pain shoots through my right palm as it slams against the stone to hard and twists at an unnatural angle.

A yelp escapes my throat and I sink to the ground with a shuddering sigh. Aldrick's strong hands clasp my waist and a surge of warmth thunders through me until every inch of me is humming, making me feel like I'm suspended in the air. Every muscle in me melts into his touch and I can't find the words to ask him what he's doing. He lifts me up with such ease, as though I'm made of feathers, and I'm left trembling with anticipation.

Aldrick sets me on the rim of the fountain, his hands still grasping my waist. He then draws me closer until there's no gap between us, his chin nearly grazing my forehead as I struggle to breathe. He slowly releases his right hand from my waist and delicately places it under my chin, lifting my head so our gazes meet. My body is pinned between his arm and almighty form. I am transfixed by the smoldering fire in Aldrick's eyes.

"I've had enough of waiting," he rasps, his gaze drilling into me. "I have never been patient and you're driving me crazy with need, Jane. Yet I can't do anything unless you open up to me. I can't forget all that we shared. I need your trust, as we once had.

You're my future—there was never anyone else before you. You are mine."

My heart thuds in my chest as fear, desire, and uncertainty battle it out inside me. My tongue feels thick and heavy, like a useless lump of clay that I can't move around to form a single word. I used to feel frustrated when Aldrick called me 'mate'; now the need arising from that simple word drives me wild. Before I can react, he takes a few steps back and watches me with a searing intensity, as if he's trying to gauge my feelings.

Then, without another word, he spins around and strides away, leaving me standing still with aching desires I cannot express.

But deep within, I know the truth. I want him more than I realize and now I am finally ready to admit it to myself.

CHAPTER
SIX

A candle flickers at the foot of the bed, emphasizing my nudity and rising arousal. I move my right hand between my thighs, rubbing circles against my sensitive spot while with my left hand I fondle my breasts, tugging and squeezing each nipple in an exquisite rhythm. I gasp, wanting and needing more.

A shadow appears in the corner and I recognize him instantly. "Aldrick," I whisper. "I want you to fuck me with both your cocks. I need to feel you inside me."

Aldrick's powerful roar echoes through my veins, igniting an uncontrollable fire of passion that threatens to consume me. My mouth opens around a desperate plea, words failing me as I beg him with my eyes to come closer. The heat within me is unbearable and my body writhes uncontrollably with an unquenchable desire. The darkness overwhelms me and I am unable to cope with the sheer pleasure that courses through my veins.

I hear Aldrick coming closer, his thunderous footsteps causing the floor to vibrate wildly beneath me and driving me into a state of frenzy. As he stands before me, he wraps his hand around his hardened length. I can feel his primal magnetism pulling me closer as I succumb to a pleasure like no other.

"Aldrick!" I moan as my entire body trembles in anticipation, hoping that he won't let me wait for long. "I need you inside me now. I am desperate be fucked by your enormous cocks!"

Aldrick kneels before me, his lips drawing into an impish grin. He clasps my thighs possessively, regarding me with a feral hunger. The proof of my desire rushes from my core and slides between my thighs.

He forces my legs apart, exposing before him like an offering. I bite my lip then a throaty moan escapes my lips. Aldrick lowers himself onto me and stares at my pulsating wet pussy that is desperate for his attention. All boundaries between us have been struck down. My head spins in surrender, the very core of me transforming into a languid puddle at his feet.

Aldrick breathes air into my pussy, so my entire body starts to tremble. I want his mouth on my clit and I wiggle desperately for him to move.

"You are soaking for me, Jane. Tell me how much you want me to feast on you?" he asks. His lips are only inches from mine and I need him to touch me, lick me before I lose my mind.

"Feast on it, Aldrick. Now ... please, Master," I beg and then he lets go of a groan before he buries his face in my crotch and runs his fingers over my slit. I moan and squirm for his tongue is like a sharp-ened blade that slashes and carves me up into a masterpiece of sensations.

His tongue curls and contorts, penetrating me in ways I did not know were possible, pushing me beyond my limits as one hand presses down on my waist, locking me in place. I scream and writhe in pleasure, feeling completely consumed by his lips and tongue that is now finding its way inside me. He takes over all my senses, ravaging me while I beg for more. I push myself further into him, desperate for the pleasure he brings. His fingers tighten on my waist as if to ensure I will never leave him.

My muscles stiffen and my breathing quickens as I see Aldrick's face transform into Karken's mocking smirk. His grip tightens painfully as I try to escape his grasp, but his strength is too much for me. I let out a loud, fearful shriek but Karken is undeterred. He finally pulls away and rises to face me. He wants to make me his, and I feel the tip of his cock press against my pulsating centre as he suddenly lowers himself down. He leans closer, his fetid breath washing over me. "You're mine now," he whispers, and I realize there's no escape. Karken will take me no matter what, and with a shuddering breath, I yield to him.

With a scream, I open my eyes and quickly realize it was only a dream ... followed by a nightmare. I recognize my room and I feel such relief that I'm completely alone. My nightgown sticks to my back and I try to calm my racing heart.

I curl up against my mattress, trying to forget the nightmare that flooded my mind with terror. Silence envelops the room in a suffocating grip and my heart cowers in fear as I choke back a sob. Aldrick's face flashed before me in my dream, his wicked smile almost too much to bear.

How can I still desire him even after knowing he's treacherous? The vision of Karken replaced

Aldrick and I'm jolted with a deep sense of foreboding that something sinister is arising. Then, something strange happened: it felt like more than a dream, more like a memory from my past that I somehow forgot. Could all of this be the pieces to the puzzle of my lost identity?

A chill runs down my spine as Karken appears in the midst of the chaos, a beacon of hope to rescue me from Aldrick's clutches. Is something else at work here, pushing me away from Aldrick and toward something else? I need to know what is going on because I am not in control of this situation. These monsters have so many secrets, ones I cannot seem to unravel until I find myself.

But how?

I throw myself out of bed and stalk around the room like a caged animal, my mind a maelstrom of questioning and dread. How can I possibly understand what is happening when every part of me is drawn to these creatures?

I feel cornered and helpless, desperately trying to make sense of Aldrick's intentions and Karken's true motives. The only thing that keeps the terror at bay is my determination to break free from their influence and start a life away from them. The faint voice in the back of my head warns me that I must find a way out of Mount Moorhead before it's too late.

I'm transfixed by the unyielding, thunderous rattle that echoes from the door in front of me. My skin prickles as a primal instinct kicks in and my veins pump with adrenaline, ready for fight or flight. Panic floods my mind and I'm overwhelmed by my feelings. But then a rush of courage graces me with its comfort. I take a deep breath and grip the door-knob until my knuckles whiten, readying myself for whatever lies beyond. Then, with one final exhale, I turn the knob.

"I hope I didn't wake you," Lena says, standing outside the door, her beauty so mesmerizing that it takes my breath away. Her tiny-waisted figure is perfect, and she looks like one of those people who never have to watch what they eat. Her striking purple dress with a dark blue sash cinched around her waist, gives her an hourglass silhouette. She gives me the warmest and most genuine smile I've seen in a while, making me feel like I'm looking into the sun.

"No," I say quickly when I realize I might have been staring for too long. "I have been up for a while. Do you want to come in?"

"Yes, I do," she says.

When I step aside to let her in, she storms into the room like an avenging angel. Her eyes dart around like a hawk and her hands are clenched into fists as she steps forward, her footfalls echoing like thunder. She stops before the flower vases, her body rigid with rage. Grasping the first one, she lifts it to her breast, a motion that releases a wave of heat that singes me where I am standing. I hear Lena's heavy breathing as her internal storm rages on, the energy that radiates from her almost threatening to consume everything in its path.

"Can I help you with something?" I ask, concerned.

She turns to me, now exuding the calm and friendliness I have come to expect from her. The vase in her hands reflects the warm light from the window.

"This used to be my room," she says, her voice taking on a slightly sharp edge, "And I'm not sure how I feel about Aldrick putting you here while also turning it into a sanctuary for our dead siblings."

She seems so distraught but she holds her composure.

"I had no idea this was your room," I whisper.

Lena glares at the vase then places it back on the shelf, struggling to control her trembling hands as each movement must be exact and precise. Her mind floods with vivid memories that dissolve her carefully crafted composure.

She turns to me again and speaks through gritted teeth, "My brother wanted this room for himself like some sort of trophy. He was never content with his own chambers, three times the size of it. He'd hunt and then force our father to hang up the heads of whatever creatures he killed on my walls—something about him being the heir or some other nonsense that I never cared for. I just wanted my own space, somewhere I could be free from his intrusions, but they refused to let me have that."

I try to fill the void of silence and offer a feeble response, "Sounds like you two wouldn't have gotten along as children." Lena's face softens and a genuine smile brightens it as if she is reliving fond memories. "It was nothing like that. We were each other's best friends. He just liked to get on my nerves sometimes," she says. With a graceful swagger that more resembles a runway model than an old woman, she strides toward me.

Her eyes scan the room as if the walls could speak and tell her stories of what has happened in this very room for decades. She stops in front of me and her vexed gaze throws me for a loop. "Do you think that you are the first human girl he's kept locked up in this very room, wearing those dresses?"

"Locked up?" I bite off the last word and my stomach twists. "I am not a prisoner," I insist, trying not to raise my voice. "I am here because I choose to stay until I regain my memories." My words hang in the air like thick smoke that refuses to disperse and clogs up the atmosphere. The oppressive and looming fog will not be shifted as if it is made out of pure steel, weighing down heavily on us.

Lena's brows clench together and her lips twitch as though she is trying to contain a flood of laughter. Is she mocking me? Then, she turns and strides toward the grand painting on the far wall. "What magnificent artwork..." she whispers feverishly.

Lena returns to me with purpose in her step. The air between us is charged with uncertainty, my throat threatening to close up. Panic courses through me as I search desperately for words to respond with. But before I can even open my mouth to offer some explanation, Lena looms over me, and I swallow hard. "You're a beautiful girl, Jane," she whispers, brushing my cheek delicately with her left hand. "I just hope you make the right decision."

Lena then moves toward the door, while I grapple with the meaning of her words. I am not ready to make any decision yet. I remain rooted to the spot in shock until her voice calls out from the doorway. I note her cold, steely eyes and my heart plummets when she utters the damning words: "Ask Aldrick about Caroline. His face will surely blanch at the mention. Let's see if he can offer any plausible explanation."

A wave of rage and betrayal rises in me like a storm as Lena disappears from sight. Karken and Khimaira's murky motivations become sharp and defined in comparison to what is going on in Lena's head. Her goal is unclear, but somehow I feel she's here to manipulate me. So much for thinking we could be friends...

Broken shards of the trust and faith I had started to have in her cut deep, spilling my confidence and leaving me questioning the world around me. It has only been one day and I'm surrounded by strangers. Aldrick could be just as much of a liar. With every passing second, my suspicions threaten to corrode every last shred of hope.

I hastily grab the book Aldrick has given me and bolt for the door, hoping to avoid another volley of Lena's intrusive questions. The hallway beyond my room is empty and I briefly exhale in relief before realizing that Teon is blocking my way.

I clench my fists at my side and meet his gaze with a fiery intensity. "I need to see Aldrick," I demand, my voice dripping with determination. "I don't have the time or energy to argue with you." Knox and Teon's eyes widen as they understand I'm not asking for permission. "Take me to him," I demand, and Teon exchanges passing looks with his brothers.

My fists curl into tight balls of rage, my fingernails biting into my palms. "I need to do this. I need to speak with him," I hiss through clenched teeth.

Teon's brow furrows. "I can't. He's with his brother and they are having an important discussion. We can't interrupt them."

But I'm already storming past them, intent on getting what I need from Aldrick, no matter the cost.

My anger rises like a flaming volcano and I take a deep breath, attempting to calm down. "Fine," I snap, feeling perfectly stoic. "Tell Aldrick that I now remember how to leave this castle and I'm finally done with this place—forever!"

I stare Teon straight in the eye. "It is through the wall down the corridor," I state. His eyes widen for I am right—I have finally remembered the way out of here and he wouldn't be able to stop me, even if he tried. "Take me to Aldrick or I'm going to simply walk away and go back to the world I know because surely, this can't be my future. And trust me when I say that you won't be able to stop me. No one can."

His body tenses, knowing full well that if he decides to fight, it will not be a battle he will easily win.

"Fine, let's go, but this won't be on me," he mutters, taking a step back. He finally turns around and we start walking to the stairs. I'm fed up with waiting for the answers and I'm ready to take action to confront Aldrick and find out the truth.

My heart is pounding and my hands shake uncontrollably as I recall the plan I've mulled over to escape this castle. When my memories came through, I realized the depth of Aldrick's deception. I'd put my trust in him, believing he would keep his word and free me. When I fled the first time it was not because I missed my world but because he was determined to keep me here.

Something else stirred within me, an over-whelming whirlwind of emotions that I could not bring myself to quash. My hope burned brightly while I was desperate for Aldrick to share his truth, yet he remained distant and silent, shrouding his intentions in mystery.

I've been stuck in this monster of a castle for

days and I've had it. Lena laughed at me, mocking my sense of freedom no doubt, yet the truth is, I can't stay in a place where I'm bound by someone else's rules and orders.

Moments later, Teon and I stand in front of a door to a room I've yet to enter. Aldrick's servant watches me intently, but he knows better than to speak out against me. The three of them should have made an effort because I hate when people keep things from me.

I'm done following instructions like a puppet on a string, done with being treated as if I'm made of glass. I'm a strong and independent woman who is ready to make her voice heard. Nothing will keep me from taking action, not even a giant like Aldrick.

CHAPTER
SEVEN

A mess of nerves, I cautiously open the door. As I step inside the dim room, the air carries with it Aldrick's scent. I wonder why these monsters like the darkness so much. I sense his powerful energy emanating from the walls, making my stomach churn with so many conflicting emotions.

The room is enormous, with a lofty ceiling criss-crossed by arched, wooden beams. Ancient portraits in gold-plated frames hang on the walls, depicting men wearing crowns that had been passed down through many generations. A grandiose, circular table occupied the center of the space, radiating power—the same power that had been used to make crucial decisions in the past.

I finally notice Aldrick and Karken sitting at the table with Khimaira perched on Karken's lap. Annoyance nags at me at the sight. I get the sudden urge to turn around and leave, but I am miffed enough to see this through, so I brace myself.

I stop in front of their table, wondering what the hell is going on here. I gasp in shock when Khimaira shifts and I finally realize Karken being serviced by her, who is now on her knees, her mouth moving over his erect cock. His fingers are tangled in her hair while Aldrick has pieces of paper spread out in front of him, his focus decidedly on whatever conundrum he was trying to solve.

What the fuck?

"Hello, Jane," Karken moans, closing his eyes as he is enjoying what Khimaira is doing to him. "How nice of you to join this party."

"What the hell is going on here, Aldrick?" I ask, horrified that Khimaira is not stopping even when it is obvious I entered the room. Is this a common thing in Moorhead, getting sucked off by your mate while other people are present? Well, I don't think I would ever become accustomed to their culture.

"What do you mean?" Aldrick asks in confusion. "You shouldn't be here, Jane."

"Really, and why is that?" I ask sternly, folding

my arms over my chest. I can see Karken's smile widen from my peripheral vision although I am not sure if it is as a result of what I said or because Khimaira has quickened the up and down movement of her head down his shaft. "Never mind, don't answer that. I want to know what you and your siblings are doing using me as some kind of ammunition to fight whatever battles you have going on among you."

Aldrick narrows his eyes looks up at me. He is most certainly annoyed by my statement. I know that I have definitely pushed his buttons so I prepare myself for whatever response he will give me.

Meanwhile, Karken's moans get progressively louder—that clown is clearly mocking Aldrick and me, and while Aldrick appears to be unfazed by it, it is hard for me to ignore. I wonder if his bother has two cocks too and if all the monsters on Moorhead have similar appendages.

"I have no idea what you're talking about, Jane, but none of this should be your concern so I suggest that you return to your room and stay out of my business," Aldrick says, each word laced with palpable infuriation. My jaw drops and I can't believe that he just spoke to me in such a condescending manner in front of his brother and his mate.

"Who is Caroline?" I ask, and the room goes silent and still all of a sudden. Color drains from Aldrick's face as his blue eyes darken. Karken and Khimaira finally stop what they're doing and Khimaira raises her head slowly, as though this is an interaction she does not want to miss. Behind Aldrick, a figure moves in the shadows and Lena emerges from behind a pillar with that damned smile of hers pasted on her face. I'm even more in shock now than I was before. Clearly, she has been in the room the entire time while Khimaira was servicing her own brother. I find this highly inappropriate and wrong. I don't think I would ever get used to it.

"Jane," Aldrick says, looking down at the table in a bid to conceal the anger I can feel oozing out of him. "Please return to your room."

"Not before you tell me who Caroline is," I say, not planning to move at all.

"Who told you that name?" he asks, still not looking up from the table.

I chuckle at his reaction to my question. Somehow, my own resolve in the face of his anger surprises me. Maybe it is because I now know more than he thinks I know and I am ready to use my own memories as a weapon if the need arises. "What does it matter who told me that name? She is clearly important to you, otherwise you wouldn't be that affected."

"Jane, last time I'm saying this. You need to return to your room," he repeats himself, his gaze fixed on those damn papers.

"And I'll say this again: I'm not going anywhere until you tell me the truth. I have no reason to trust you now. You withhold information from me and when I ask questions, you don't answer them. Am I a prisoner? Am I truly your mate or am I just another human girl you are holding here with some sinister power?"

"Don't push me, Jane. Otherwise I'm going to take you over my knee and spank you," he growls and I back away from him. Did he just threaten to spank me? Damn it, why do I think I would enjoy such a degrading punishment? My wild, traitorous imagination sparks back to life in the most inappropriate moments. "Please return to your room and I will come to you to answer all your questions."

"Tell me now in front of your siblings," I say, stuttering a little. "They are the only ones who can tell when you're lying."

"Fine," he says, finally looking up at me, his eyes red with anger. "Caroline was another human woman. I was attracted to her. I wanted her to be my mate so badly even though I knew that she was not. I made a mistake and lost her."

"But you gained a painting." Lena chuckles from behind Aldrick, fully coming out of the shadows and standing right next to him.

"A painting?" I ask.

Aldrick lets out a deep breath and suddenly, his anger morphs into something else: discomfort. "The painting in your room. It was her work."

"You mean the painting I tried to burn?" I ask, the memory rearing its head at the right time.

Shock now registers on Aldrick's face. He has no idea just how much I remember now and to hear me mention one of our first tense moments before I even grew to like him at all must feel like being hit with a sledgehammer. "Yes," he says. "That painting."

"Right before you promised to set me free and then you threw me in a dungeon," I say.

"Jane," he says with another growl that sends a shiver down my spine. "What you remember are bits of a big picture. Do not make any hasty decisions."

"You threw me in a dungeon," I repeat with

renewed anger. "You took away my freedom because you wanted to make me your mate."

"I did not want to make you my mate. You *are* my mate. We are destined to be together," he says with absolute confidence and I want to laugh in his face. He cannot be serious.

"You told me all your siblings were dead," I keep going. "You told me they were killed during that human invasion. You jailed me for touching a bunch of flower vases."

"Get out before I lose my temper! We will talk about this another time," he roars as he stands to his feet.

I stumble backward at his action but quickly regain my stance and face him again. I have already gone so far with this confrontation. I cannot afford to turn back now.

"Or what? Are you going to throw me in the dungeon again?" Aldrick appears to be so stunned by my words as well as my stubbornness that for the first time since I have known him, he seems to be short of words. So I continue to talk. "Every time I want to leave, I get drawn back to you. I thought you were telling the truth and that I am your mate and the connection we have is because of that. Now I know you are a liar and manipulator. You wish to turn me into another Caroline and you do not care if I die in the process. But I will not let you do that. I will do all I can to break whatever spell you have cast on me and I will walk out of here alive and well. You shall see."

Of my four audience members, Aldrick is the only one who looks baffled while the other three seem highly amused by my sudden outburst, but I truly don't care. After I let it all out, I simply turn around and walk out of the room. They can have their meetings and talks—I no longer care. It's time to move on.

I steadily pick up my pace, my shoes tapping against the stone floor as my steps hasten to a vigorous march. A cold draft I never noticed before drifted through the hall, making me shiver. For a fleeting moment, I consider looking back but quickly dismiss the thought. There is no point in dwelling in the past.

When I decided I got far enough from that room, I immediately release a sigh of relief and let my body slump against the nearest wall. My hands tremble and my heart starts to race. All of the tension and fear that has been keeping me from speaking my mind has just been released, and it is both satisfying and troubling.

"I think you should get back to your room. Trust me, Jane. This is for your own good," Herb suggests gently. I'm not sure if he was around when I left the room or if he joined me while I was out, but either way, he's beside me now. I can't see his face, but his tone of voice implies that he must know something about my altercation with his master. Yet, despite this, he probably means well like the other two servants, so I need to stop being so stubborn and regroup.

The dizziness is not going away. My whole body is trembling and beads of sweat roll down my back. I don't feel well at all. Something is wrong. When I take a few steps toward the door, I stumble.

"Jane, are you okay?" Herb asks worriedly. When I try to look at him, it feels like the hallway is turning upside down.

"Oh, n-no," I say, unable to walk further and still holding on to the wall for support. I try to take another step but completely lose my balance, and since the wall has no bars I can hold on to, I fall down on my ass.

"Jane!" Aldrick's voice sounds so distant that I think my mind is playing tricks on me. But when I try to focus my eyes while on the floor, leaning on the wall, I can't see a thing. Then he appears right in front of me but like everything else, his body looks warped to me. It feels like I have taken some powerful psychoactive drug and my body is rebelling.

"What is happening to her?" I hear him ask. Even with how I am feeling, his voice is powerful enough to pierce my consciousness as sharply as crystal.

"She fell while I was accompanying her to her room. It looks like she has trouble with her balance, so this must have something to do with her ear," Herb says. By now, my vision has become so blurry that I cannot see him at all. The only person I still see is Aldrick and it is only because of his large stature which simply cannot be missed. "We should take her to her room and let her rest. She must lie down, Master Aldrick."

The next thing I feel is big arms wrapped around me and lifting me off the floor. From the immediate comfort and protection they provide, I do not need to be told who it is. Yet despite obviously needing and liking this support, I still have some protest left in me.

"Put me down, Aldrick," I manage to say, and when I try to push myself off him, I find my muscles are not so strong.

"Stay still, Jane," he says. "Let me take care of you."

Maybe it is his words or the fact I am feeling weaker and dizzier with every passing moment, but I do allow myself to relax against him and let him carry me. I do not open my eyes again until I feel him lay me gently on the bed. When my head rests against the pillow, he brushes wayward strands of my hair away from my face and covers me up with the sheets.

"I will never let anything happen to you," Aldrick says, and that is the last thing I hear before my eyes shut and I fall into the darkness.

CHAPTER
EIGHT

My eyes flick open and the light sears into my vision, bringing with it a sensation of familiarity. All the dizziness, headache and chills have evaporated, leaving me feeling as though I have been born again. Though I cannot believe how quickly the recovery process has happened, I am thankful for the feeling of strength that now fills me. I may not know exactly how long I have been unconscious, but I revel in the newfound sense of renewal that courses through my veins.

All the events leading up to my unconsciousness in Aldrick's arms come cascading back over me, as well as every lie he told and every truth revealed. I remember his strong arms picking me up off the hallway floor and bringing me to this room. With a surge of hope, I push my head off the pillow, antici- pating his presence. But no, I'm alone. Disappoint- ment fills me and a voice in my head says, 'Thanks for saving me, but you still can't be trusted.'

I pull the sheets off me and leave the bed, stretching my arms. As I put my shoes on, the door opens and I turn around to see Herb, Teon, and Knox walk into the room.

"It seems you have recovered. You gave us all a scare, Jane," Herb says cheerfully.

"Guess I am much stronger than most people here think," I say with a shrug. I don't know what happened earlier but I don't want to think about this now, while my stomach growls. I don't remember the last time I had a proper meal.

All three of them barely react to my self- affirming statement as they approach me.

"Your total disregard for nutrition is concerning, Jane," Herb scolds, and I am surprised that he is taking that kind of tone with me.

"You haven't eaten properly since you got here and you're fragile. We all believe you passed out yesterday because you haven't been fueling your body with enough food. After your bath, you will eat a rich breakfast and we don't want to hear any objections." Teon's warning tone echoes in the silence, underscoring the gravity of their plea.

I force a weak nod, struggling to agree with the condemning voice of my captors. My appetite has become foreign to me as if I have been cursed, leaving me unable to stomach anything more than stale breadcrumbs. They seem content with my answer, so they exit the room to go prepare breakfast. Obviously they mean well and they are all worried about me, especially after last night.

I start putting my clothes on and tuck my shirt in. Every button, each cut and seam is my armor against the unknown. My mind races with questions that creep up from the depths of my consciousness: What is Aldrick's agenda? Will I be able to trust anyone ever again? As if on cue, Herb and Teon reappear at my door like specters come to haunt me.

"Your breakfast is ready," Teon announces.

When I get to the dining room, I eye the table laden with food, my mouth watering as I imagine how good everything will taste. The desire to stuff myself is real, but I quash it immediately. Any time I think of my current predicament, a wave of nausea washes over me and all appetite disappears.

"No," I say firmly, finally summoning the

courage to look at them. "I don't want anything to eat."

"Jane," Herb says sternly. "You must eat something."

My eyes blaze with defiance even though my stomach is rumbling in protest.

"No," I repeat through gritted teeth. "I am not hungry anymore."

This is a total lie, but for some reason, despite the hunger, I have no appetite. I struggle to hear what the servants are saying, but the words blur together until they transform to white noise. I don't want to give them the satisfaction of a response, so I stay silent and just hope they will stop badgering me. They eventually leave me alone in my room again, and I collapse onto my bed in relief. Happiness comes over me because I know they won't be bothering me anymore. I need some time to think about my situation and decide what to do next.

Suddenly, the door opens and I sit up on the bed, feeling slightly dizzy as I do so. When my eyes focus, I find Aldrick standing there with an expression of genuine concern. I tear my gaze from him and bury my face in the sheets.

"I hear you have not been eating," he says.

"I'm not hungry," I reply, my words muffled.

"Get up. Come with me," he says in that tone that tells me there is no room for argument. He walks out of the room, leaving the door wide open. I raise my head with the intention to scream after him that I'm not going anywhere but when I see him walking down the corridor, I groan and drag myself off the bed.

Aldrick suddenly stops walking and I know he has sensed me following him. Even in the faint light of the lamps, I can make out a smug expression on his face—he's relishing every second of power he has over me.

"Where are you taking me?" I ask him.

He pushes a door on his right open and steps aside, gesturing for me to walk through. I wait for him to answer my question and when he sees my stubbornness, his face softens and he succumbs. "Just walk through the door, Jane. I have a surprise for you."

I steel myself as I walk in and hold my breath when I finally make it to the balcony. The view is breathtaking, a sweeping panorama of dense green forests cascading into an awe-inspiring waterfall that sparkles in the morning sun. The air is thick with the sounds of birds chirping and the river roaring below. But what draws my eye like a magnet is the tray on a mat set up next to the banister. My breakfast awaits me, a feast of tantalizing aromas and inviting colors— enough to overwhelm even my hardened heart.

It seems that Aldrick truly wants me to eat again. Warmth spreads over my chest. I feel a little overwhelmed because he put a lot of effort into this. He obviously cares about me.

"Aldrick, this is amazing," I say in wonder.

"You are not going to starve yourself to death on my watch," he says.

I take a few steps to the banister and hold on to it as I properly take in the view in front of me. When I take a deep breath, I smile as the gentle breeze fills my nostrils and calms my insides.

"You've never seen this place before," Aldrick says as he steps beside me by the banister. "Not even when you came here the first time."

"Oh," I say. "It must be a really special place."

"It is. It is where I came to get away from my siblings and all their troubles when we were younger."

"Tell me about your family," I say, half-expecting him to refuse but hoping that the power of the moment would soon change his mind so he'd start opening up to me.

"Eat your food and I'll tell you something with every bite you take," he says with a mischievous smile.

Rolling my eyes in disdain, I step back and slump onto the mat. All Aldrick had to do was let me appreciate the view and tantalizing aroma of the food. Instead, he has to ruin it by trying to bribe me.

Sitting directly across from me, he watches me take the first bite. My taste buds explode with flavor and for a moment, I completely forget about Aldrick's presence until he opens his mouth again. After gulping down the juice, I meet his gaze. A maelstrom of tingly bubbles pop just below the surface of my skin.

"You have met Lena and my brother. Besides them, I have another brother who mostly does not involve himself in my affairs like those other two," he says.

"Are Karken and Lena always like that? They seem slightly judgmental."

"They mean well," he says with a fond smile. "All they do is in our collective best interest."

As I eat, Aldrick tells me all about growing up in the castle. He speaks about his mother, who he loved very much, and his father, who was a brave warrior and taught him everything he knew. In return, I told him about my own family in the mortal world, the fact I was an only child and my parents had passed, and about some past experiences with my ex, Brad.

"That man hasn't treated you well at all, yet you still went back to his world. I'm thinking of breaking every bone in his body," Aldrick barks, his eyes gleaming with danger. I laugh, but then realize that he's completely serious. Luckily, he's probably never going to leave this mountain, so for now I don't have to worry about him murdering my ex.

After that, he keeps reminding me that we had some of these discussions before and he knows me far more than I think.

As I glance up at Aldrick while savoring my last bite of food, he comes across like a magnificent creature from a hidden realm. His imposing stature and horns give him an air of power and strength, and his two cocks beckon me with promises of delightful pleasure. When he offers his hand for me to rise, a current of need passes between us as our palms touch.

"Wait a second," I say as I walk back to the banister to look at the waterfall. "There are people out there. Humans!"

"Yes," Aldrick says with a chuckle. They are at a distance but I can clearly see a family of humans swimming in the river at the base of the waterfall. "Mortals come here often when the weather is good and they do climb the mountain. They cannot see this castle though. Magic has always protected us."

"This is crazy," I say, finding it hard to believe that this castle and especially this balcony, which are clearly in plain view, cannot be seen by mortals, as Aldrick calls them. In that instant, the idea of returning to the real world doesn't appeal to me at all.

"There's a complicated ancient spell that protects us from being seen by them," he explains casually.

"If I scream, they won't hear me?" I ask.

"No, they won't," he says then he gives me a sideways glance. "You can scream for me when I make love to you in your chamber later on."

Heat envelopes my cheeks and I swallow hard, struggling to push the images of him fucking me with his two cocks away, but the heat from his body feels like a drug, bonding me to him. I clear my throat and then as he walks me back to my room with my stomach full, I ask questions about all the things I have seen around, which his servants have refused to provide answers to.

Aldrick's voice dispenses words and stories,

setting me at ease. When he reaches my door and says goodbye, a new urge boils inside of me, begging me to make him stay longer, to keep talking and unlock the hidden gems of his soul. My smile stretches so wide, it hurts. Aldrick is much more than what meets the eye and I can barely contain my excitement for what else lies beneath this mysterious man-beast.

CHAPTER

NINE

I jerk awake, my heart hammering in my chest. A deafening crack of thunder shakes the castle to its core and I scream in terror. Sweat slicks my skin, mingling with the rain that pours through the cracks in the walls as lightning illuminates the room like a strobe light. I can feel the ground rumbling beneath me, as if it's alive and angry, ready to swallow us whole. This storm is no natural occurrence—it's pure wickedness made manifest. The castle may not survive this abomination. The strong howls and rumbles claw fiercely against the walls of my bedroom.

The darkness of the night seems to swell and grow around me, each clap of thunder and flash of lightning intensifying my mounting terror. I have to concentrate on keeping my breathing steady and slow, but soon enough, I am completely overwhelmed by anxiety.

Tears well in my eyes as I take small, labored breaths in bursts, knowing that this could be the last night of safety for me—the night that I might not survive. At least, that's what it feels like.

Just then, the door swings open. My first thought is that somebody is about to attack me during this storm when I will be unable to scream for help, so I shift backward on the bed, which only compounds my panic. But as my eyes focus on the figure by the door, I recognize the horns, the eyes, and the build.

"I sensed your fear, Jane, and I thought you might be struggling to sleep tonight," Aldrick says.

My throat constricts, trapping my voice in its hold. I gasp for air as a silent scream escapes me. Aldrick notices my visible distress and immediately moves to the bed, engulfing me in his strong embrace. He whispers soothing words in my ear as he tenderly strokes my hair.

"It's all right," he reassures me. "Just stay calm. It'll be over before you know it."

I worry that his iron-clad embrace will cause more harm than good, yet his skin against mine and his alluring scent fills my senses and begins to soothe me. He continues to brush my hair and stroke my back until my heartbeat relaxes and my breathing stabilizes. Even when it seems like I am okay, he does not let go. Rather, he lowers us both onto the bed, wrapping his arms around me like a protective blanket. With all of the fear dissipating, I drift off comfortably into sleep in this comforting embrace.

I DIP my body into the pool and let the cool water wash over me. My mind is preoccupied with thoughts of Aldrick, from his gentle touch to our tumultuous days together. He has been gone since I woke up this morning and asking around has only revealed that he is busy tending to his own affairs. Though I yearn for us to be together once more, I know better than to demand anything of him. Aching with desire, I stay in the pool until it no longer brings me solace. I am eager to touch myself, but I quickly abandon that thought. I want him to use my body as he sees fit because this will be much more satisfying.

I have no idea how many days have passed, but

with my memory returning, and his utter care of me in my worst moments, my feelings for him have gained wings...

My thoughts are interrupted by the sound of giggles coming from behind me. I hear Karken and Khimaira's laughter echoing through the dark corridors of the castle. Without a second thought, I grab the nearest piece of clothing I can find, a towel, and wrap it around myself. Stealthily I follow their trail until they finally emerge from the garden into an overgrown walkway that seems like a maze with lush ferns and mossy walls.

My heart races as I pick up my pace and eventually make it higher up the mountain, following them outside into the open air. The exhilaration of discovery pumps through my veins as I take in the sight before me. Ignoring the twigs and pebbles cutting into my feet, I hide behind a big rock and watch as Karken and Khimaira stand at the edge of the mountain. I don't think they are here to simply admire the view. For starters, it is dark and not an ideal time to appreciate one's surroundings.

It is clear from the start that they intend to do more than just stare at the world ahead. They start kissing, their mouths fumbling with impatience and passion. Karken and Khimaira's passionate embrace is electric, fueled by an unquenchable desire. The clothes they wear are barely a barrier between them and they quickly discard them and toss them on the ground.

Karken's hard body lies exposed with heavy, erect cocks and Khimaira's perky nipples bear faint red marks from his roughly exploring hands. He drags his lips across her neck and she visible shivers while she reaches to his thick cocks, which start ... vibrating.

My jaw drops. I can hardly believe what I am seeing. He starts teasing her wet slit and she moans, telling him to stick it in deep inside her. I feel a little apprehensive about watching them, but their energy pulses, so strong, and the air smells of sex and sweat. In all honesty, I ache to have the same experience with Aldrick.

My throat goes dry when suddenly, Khimaira says something to Karken and he obeys without question. It seems like she's the one in control in this moment. Karken lies patiently as she climbs on top of him, then trails her pelvis all the way from his thighs to his face.

Then, she begins to move slowly against his mouth, her hands tugging on his hair. My breath catches in shock when she reaches for his face and

Karken responds by stretching out his impossibly long tongue and exploring her entire body with it, like an expert sculptor molding a masterpiece. He caresses her all over, giving her pleasure. Each curl of his tongue on all the sensitive spots seems to drive her closer to the edge. She grips his hair tighter, moaning loudly and arching her back.

Then, he uses his tongue to fuck her and I can't stop staring.

If only I could ever experience a fraction of what Karken's tongue is providing... My right hand instinctively slides beneath my towel and I feverishly rub my throbbing clit, imagining how a talented tongue like that can bring me closer to an earth-shattering climax. I am sucked into a battle between pleasure and pain until all that exists is the universe between my legs.

A throaty whisper slips over my shoulder, sending a chill down my spine, and I know it's Aldrick without even turning around. His large body looms behind mine, blocking out all of the light around us. His presence electrifies my veins, my hands tremble with desire as I slowly turn around to meet his gaze. In one swift motion, he embraces me, trapping me in the circle of his arms as if caging an animal. My skin tingles with arousal as his hot breath caresses my neck. He holds me there as I watch Karken and Khimaira in front of us, unable to move or look away.

Khimaira eagerly slides down Karken's body, taking both of his cocks in her mouth at the same time. She bends and contorts—it truly looks as if her mouth can stretch beyond its limits to accommodate him.

Aldrick seizes my arm and tugs me to him without warning, once again guiding my hand back to where it was just a moment before. The heaviness of anticipation and need floods through my veins until I'm sure I will burst. Aldrick's erection presses over my buttocks, the size of it making my mouth go dry.

Aldrick then takes control of my hand, pushing my fingers into my wet slit. I gasp and almost scream out from the intensity, but before a sound escapes Aldrick smothers it with his other hand, covering my lips.

Karken's grunts fill the air and mingle with Khimaira's moans as she massages him with her hands. The pleasure that radiates through me grows unbearable so I bite down hard on Aldrick's hand and cry out, nearly blinded the shattering orgasm as he continues to fuck me with my own fingers. I'm lost in the power of sensation as I come again and again, him holding me tightly, promising that this is just the beginning.

MY SLEEP IS SUDDENLY SHATTERED by the sound of my bedroom door creaking open, and I jolt awake with a hope that it might be Aldrick on the other side. But instead of seeing the man I so desperately desire, reality sets in as the now revealing light of the morning sun illuminates Lena standing in my doorway, an all too familiar smug grin across her face.

"Hello, Jane," she says as she walks into the room, uninvited. "You made us all so worried."

"Why?" I ask, not sure if she knows what happened to me a few days ago. Maybe she has seen me passing out in the hallway. "Sorry to make you all so worried."

"How are you feeling now?" she asks, walking past me in the same determined manner she did the last time she came in and told me to ask Aldrick about Caroline.

An unpleasant feeling coils in my stomach like a snake and all I can think about is how this woman is still trying to manipulate me. Has she intentionally aimed to cause a rift between Aldrick and me by making me ask him those questions? What does she plan to tell me next that would only add more distance between us? Her intentions are a mystery, but I have a feeling none of this is good.

"What do you want?" I ask her, slightly startling her so she stops midway into the room and turns around to face me. She stares at me impassively, her skin as pale as a ghost's and lips the color of blood. I am transfixed by her icy gaze.

"You are not Aldrick's mate," she says. "You are just another Caroline and my brother is too stubborn and blind to realize that."

Lena's words hang in the air like a thick fog, smothering both of us. My blood boils as we remain locked in an uncomfortable silence. With her piercing gaze drilling into me, I have no choice but to confront her. "Was this your plan all along? To drive a wedge between your brother and me?"

"Your narcissism is astounding," she says with a scoff. "It makes me wonder what the deal is with you."

"I am not his mate, you're right. And there's no deal with me. What you see is what you get..."

"Everything I have done has been to show you the truth," she says, loud enough to drown out my own words. "I did not lie to you, did I? I just led you to find out yourself how you are being tricked."

"So, what do you want now?" I ask with a shrug, trying to act like her words don't affect me. "Why are you telling me all this?"

She scoffs again and rolls her eyes. "I have my own choices for him. Females who do not carry that human stench that you have soiled this castle with."

I stare at Lena in disbelief and disgust, digesting the truth of her nature. She has pretended to be my friend with her saccharine smiles and honeyed words, yet it was simply a deceitful front to manipulate me into believing she was on my side. She is nothing but a conniving harlot who has loathed me at first sight. Sure, she may have pushed me toward finding out the secrets Aldrick has lied about or kept hidden from me, but her intentions were anything but benevolent. All she wants is to satisfy her own selfish interests and eliminate me. I can't help but question who she intends Aldrick to mate with.

"I would start to gather my things and say my goodbyes if I were you," she says as she retraces her steps to the door. "Your time in this castle has come to an end."

TEN

As Lena stalks out the door, my chest swells with an overpowering emotion—a passionate aversion to being driven away from this castle which I have called home for a while. Despite all I have said about staying away, I cannot help but feel like Aldrick and I have so much more to explore together, if only I can stay and find out what fate has in store for us. I think I am finally ready for him to take control and show me what I have been missing out on all this time. I wish I told him last night to take me back to his chambers and have his way with me ... to fuck me until I couldn't walk.

I stand in the empty hallway, trembling with

anger and anxiety. My first instinct is to sprint to Aldrick for protection, but that will be foolish. Lena may be a monster, but Aldrick is no saint. If I go to him now, it will mean admitting defeat and accepting his lies. No, I need to find someone else in this den of snakes who has power and can help me unravel the truth.

I take the first step forward, knowing full well that every move I make could be my last in this world. With each step I take down the dark corridor, I feel like I am venturing deeper into a labyrinth filled with traps and threats hiding in the shadows. But I can't stop now. I must find someone who can help me fight against these monsters or die trying.

I tiptoe past Aldrick's door in a state of complete terror, as if I'm peering into the gates of Hell. I almost expect to feel his cold, powerful grip on my arm or hear his callous voice ordering me to stop. Thankfully, I manage to pass by his chambers.

When I finally reach Karken's door, it feels like the entrance to an unknown abyss filled with hidden dangers. My heart races as I contemplate what I'm about to do— a decision that could change the course of fate and either bring joy or danger in its wake. I know deep down that Karken isn't much better than Aldrick, and he too is on a mission to ensure a specific individual becomes his brother's mate.

The looming terror that Lena brings will soon be upon me and if I am to survive this without succumbing to Karken's machinations, then the only way is forward. With my knuckles, I rap against the door twice, with a force that belies the quaking fear inside me.

The door swings open in one swift movement to reveal Karken standing on the other side. My breath hitches in my throat because he's practically naked. His entire upper body is exposed, revealing bulging muscles, carved and ridged to perfection with beads of sweat rolling over them. Underneath it, I can see the heads of his cocks glistening and their shafts threatening to rip the cloth of his pants to shreds. Behind him, his tail is swinging furiously and it is the first time I am seeing it.

Oh dear, I'm showing up at the worst of times...

Karken's eyes blaze with a fiery rage as he glares around the room, ready to unleash his wrath on whoever has disrupted his peace. His muscles bulge and tense under his skin as his fists curl. When my gaze meets his, he startles before softening. He straightens up and plants his feet firmly on the floor, looking down at me with a challenge posed in one arched eyebrow, daring me to look away from him.

"I've been waiting for you, Jane," he says, his eyes darkening.

I clear my throat. "Do you have a moment to talk?"

"Who is it, my love?" Khimaira's voice comes from inside his chambers, causing Karken to make a quarter turn toward her and giving me some space to be able to look into the room. My gaze falls upon the sight of her sprawled out naked on the bed in the center, her limbs spread wide invitingly. Her full breasts are plump, marked with red-hot handprints that make my stomach flutter, knowing they were left by Karken's rough touch. Of course I have stumbled onto an intimate moment and I avert my gaze, looking everywhere but at her.

"This is bad timing, sorry. I will come back when ... ugh, you're less busy," I say in embarrassment.

"Nonsense. We can always make time for our Jane," he says then gestures to invite me into their space. Panic grips me and I'm not at all sure about this. I have been exposed to their wild lust, and now they glare at me with a stony silence that speaks volumes. The hairs on the back of my neck prickle as I suffer their penetrating gazes upon me.

"I can come back," I say.

"You really need to talk to us, Jane. Don't be afraid, we don't bite," Karken says, and although his expression shows amusement, his tone holds an undercurrent of gravity.

"Fine." I step in and Karken closes the door behind me. Now that I am in the room, Khimaira does not bother to cover herself up for my benefit. She remains in that position, one hand on her breasts and the other rubbing her clit gently, as though she is keeping herself stimulated for Karken.

A few feet from the bed is a small circular table around which are two chairs. I take one of the chairs and Karken takes the second. I hesitate as I gather my thoughts.

"We are listening, Jane. Don't make us wait for too long," he says impatiently.

"Okay." I standing up from the chair, causing it to make a scraping sound. I suddenly feel unwelcome now that I am in front of Karken. "Maybe this is a bad idea after all. I'll go."

"No. Sit," Karken orders as I take a few steps toward the door. "I think we can help each other. It seems there is a lot on your mind."

With a deep breath, I return to the seat. "I believe I have been played by your sister." As soon as the words leave my mouth, Karken bursts into raucous laughter. Even as I shift uncomfortably, he does not stop laughing. He seems determined to mock me and I do not blame him. I am the one who has come to him of my own volition. "This is not at all amusing to me, but go ahead and laugh at my expense."

"Oh, Jane," he says as he finally gets a hold of himself. "I'm not laughing at you. Well, at least not entirely. I just think it funny that Lena is still as devious as she always used to be. Let me guess, she is the one responsible for that outburst of yours from few days ago?"

I recoil from Karken's judgmental gaze, feeling my face heat up with shame and mortification. His words drip with disdain, making it evident that everyone is aware of Lena's conniving ways. Dread fills me as I envision his mocking laughter if I admit my gullibility, so I consider telling a white lie. But knowing I can't keep anything hidden within this small community, I decide to confess. "She told me to ask Aldrick about Caroline."

"And I suppose now that you and Aldrick are

estranged, she has her own choice of who ought to be his mate," he says casually.

"Yes," I respond, surprised that he has figured it all out so quickly and so easily. "How do you know that? And Aldrick and I have reconciled to an extent."

"This is not the first time my sister has tried to fix our brother with a mate. She fancies herself a matchmaker of sorts," he admits, shaking his head in resignation.

"Well," Khimaira says as she rises from the bed and starts to walk toward us. Despite their lack of inhibition, I still cannot get accustomed to the sight of their bare bodies. This isn't something that people do in my world, but obviously this is completely normal behaviour in Moorhead. "She did find me for you."

"Her only success," Karken says as Khimaira stops beside him and he grabs her ass with his hands.

"Can we focus?" I bark, interrupting their display of intimacy.

Khimaira glances at me in surprise but doesn't resist when Karken pulls her onto his lap. The table hides the obscene gesture he makes with his hand between her legs, but the sounds that escape her lips

SOPHIA SMUT

are unmistakable. I hate them for flaunting their lust so brazenly in front of me, yet a part of me craves that same raw passion. If only things weren't so complicated with Aldrick.

"Now, what do you want me to do for you?" Karken asks.

"I want to stay in the castle until I can be sure that I can trust Aldrick fully and also so I can get to know him a bit better," I say.

Karken searches my face as he mulls my words. I can practically feel him unraveling the truth of what I've said and piecing it together, ever so slowly, until finally it clicks into place like a puzzle. His silence is deafening but speaks volumes.

"You truly have feelings for him, do you not?" he asks.

"I'm not entirely sure," I say. "I think he is using some power to try to influence me."

Karken's lips curl up into an insidious sneer, making me want to slam my fist into his face and erase the monstrous indignation he's sporting. "Aldrick cannot do this!" he taunts, his voice dripping with a sweetness I never knew was possible from him. "You should start thinking of yourself as his mate now."

All of a sudden the web of lies has been

126

exposed, and I can clearly see who Aldrick's siblings truly are. Lena may have presented herself as kind and inviting at first, but now I understand that she is ready to bare her teeth if it means protecting what she believes is hers. In contrast, when I saw Karken and his mate for the first time, I was certain they meant mischief. Now though, I was witness to their palpable passion for one another, so strong that nothing else matters—not even me.

"Or maybe you are not and Lena will find his true mate. I truly do not care. This mate business is starting to bore me," Karken barks, interrupting my thoughts. "But I will help you do whatever you want to do about Lena. She's my sister but we never liked each other much. Maybe I'll finally get the chance to teach her a lesson once and for all."

"That's it?" I ask, surprised at his acquiescence. "I'm supposed to believe you'll help me out of the goodness of your heart? I think I know by now to not trust you people blindly. What do you stand to gain?"

"We have our own affairs to deal with, but we came to visit Aldrick to have a little break," Karken explains.

"Okay. So, what do you suggest I do?"

"Leave Lena to me. Focus on your own issues with my brother."

"Thank you, Karken," I say but he only waves me off in response, possibly because Khimaira is doing things to his cock that are making him lose the ability to speak. I turn away from them and walk straight out of the chambers without looking back.

My heart beats faster as I stand outside Karken's chambers. As I watched him and his lover, their passion burned a hole through me. My body is in serious need of a passionate touch that only Aldrick can provide. My eyes fixate on his door at the end of the hallway, my mind racing with what could be happening behind it. He is adamant we are fated mates. He's been telling me he'd only take me when I'm ready.

So, am I ready?

I imagine him spread invitingly on his bed or chair, his firm cocks proudly erect and throbbing in anticipation of our touch. If I were to enter his chambers now and find him stroking himself with alluring eyes locked onto mine, I know I will be powerless to resist. My body aches for my true mate no matter how hard I try to control it. Every cell in my being longs for him and his vibrating cocks, and if he were to touch me in the way I yearn to be touched, it would take a miracle to turn away.

Before I do anything I might regret, though, I plan to pass his door and keep going. Much like when I was coming to Karken's room, I hurry down the hall so that I can minimize the chance of running into Aldrick.

I am practically standing on Aldrick's doorstep when the door suddenly swings open and there he stands, looking like a vision of divine beauty. The shock on his face mirrors mine. I bite back a gasp, but it is too late—we have both been caught off-guard in this chance encounter.

"Jane?! I had no idea you have woken up already," he exclaims, and the deep timber of his voice seeps into my bones like burning hot magma.

I'm on fire and hungry. Not for food but for him.

"About an hour ago," I say with a steady voice, deep down thinking about last night and him pleasuring me with my own fingers. The orgasm was intense and I loved how alive he made me feel.

"How are you feeling?" he asks, striding out of his chambers.

He is inquiring about my wellbeing, yet his eyes remain distant, as if my inner turmoil doesn't faze him in the slightest.

"Better," is the only word I manage. Though my intention is to keep my responses brief and not give away how I'm feeling, he seems to sense the simmering frustration in every syllable. My chest tightens and I clench my fists, determined not to reveal the depth of my emotions.

My entire body locks up as Aldrick reaches out to me. Every rational thought exits my brain, leaving only a desperate and frantic longing that swells within me until it threatens to consume me whole. His fingers dig into my skin as he cups my face in his hands. He looms over me with a fierce intensity, stopping mere inches from my trembling lips.

"What are you doing?" I whisper.

"The real question is what you are doing to me," he asks and his eyes become wild and manic, matching the energy of my own. With every word out of his mouth, I am drowning in a wave of terror and anguish. "When you stood up to me, you excited me in ways I cannot begin to describe. I wanted to grab you and fill your mouth with my cock."

A primal urge builds within me and I open my mouth to unleash it. The words tumble forth as if begging for release from the confines of my soul. "Do it," I plead. "Make me yours, Aldrick."

The flames burn brighter down my spine until

they settle deep in my gut, urging me to reach out to him. These words I just whispered will seal our fate together.

"I have been waiting to hear you say those words," he growls, his voice thick with desire. I don't need anybody else to tell me that all my darkest cravings are about to be fulfilled, and nothing in this world can stop us now.

ELEVEN

The door slams shut behind us like a thunderous gunshot, but Aldrick's hands are relentless and hold me firmly in his grasp. He tears my dress from my body with his tongue and teeth, sending sparks of pleasure through me as he marks my neckline with deep scratches. He lifts me effortlessly into the air, cradling me as though I am weightless. His hands grip my buttocks, sending a trill of pleasure through me.

"I am going to fuck you so hard, it will take you days to recover," he seethes, and the heat of his utterances fills my being. I cannot find a single word in response—all I can do is surrender myself to him, let him consume me in a world of ecstasy.

Every cell that makes up me is hungry for his touch.

Aldrick clutches me tight against his chest as we speed toward his bed, and in a single motion he casts me onto the feathery mattress. As soon as our bodies part, I ache for him to return, so I reach out and grasp desperately at the air, begging to draw him back against me. I want us as close as can be, skin to skin.

"You know what you are begging for, Jane?" he asks me. His tone is a deep rumble that creates perceptible waves in the air that hit my body and shake me to my core.

"Yes."

The lamps in the room cast a radiant halo around his figure. I have never seen someone like this before and with him standing over me in such a way, there's not much I would be able to deny him.

Aldrick towers over me and in one swift move-ment he rips off his clothes, exposing his chiseled body for my pleasure. His legs are like carved statues that I long to be trapped between, and my gaze moves up greedily over every inch of his flawless form until our eyes lock with a sizzling intensity.

A lump forms in my throat as I take in the sight before me. Even with a dozen memories of him standing naked, nothing could have prepared me for this moment. His cock is both thick and long, powerful enough to make me quiver with just one glance. Like a flood, uncontrollable desire rushes through my veins as I realize he has another tool at his disposal, ready to be used to ravage me however he pleases. My mouth goes dry as I bask in the power of Aldrick's body.

"Do you still want me to devour you?" he asks, stroking each of his cocks with one hand and smiling at me with a devilish glint in his eyes. "I remember you told me on a few occasions that you like it rough, Jane. You like it when I nearly split you apart."

I swallow hard. "Yes, fuck me hard, Aldrick. Don't make me wait," I say, and I mean every word with every fiber of my being.

"With pleasure," he responds, his smirk deepening.

He fiercely strokes his twitching cocks, his impassive gaze locked on mine.

"Kneel in front of me, woman," he says, delivering his command like a hammer blow. His voice is thunderous and demanding, deep and unyielding.

All thought ceases and my brain turns to mush. My throat tightens, strangling my response until I manage to gasp out, "What?" with a shuddering breath.

One brow raised, he gives me a stern look and gestures at me to get up from my supine position. "Be a good girl, Jane, and get on your knees for your master."

I tremble as I kneel before him and gaze up into his eyes. His withering stare is riddled with possessive desire, and I struggle to keep my composure as my mind continues to unravel like a ball of yarn.

With his hungry gaze, a rush of adrenaline courses through me. The veins of his cocks are visibly pulsing with a feral energy. In this moment all my worries vanish, replaced by an insatiable craving to taste him. But I know that wanting something and being able to take it are two very different things.

"Such a good girl," he says in praise, me and I feel so damn pleased with myself. "You can take me into your mouth."

My eyes dart from his cocks to his eyes, which are glowing like miniature versions of the sun. "Can you read my thoughts?" I ask. He has never shown any sign of being able to do so before today but there is still so much about him and his kind that I am not privy to, and I will not be surprised if this is possible for him even if it is because we might be mates, allegedly.

"No," he states. "But your face is an open book." He puts his hand on my head and runs his fingers through my hair, massaging my scalp and slowly guiding me forward. My mouth waters with antici- pation and I squeeze my thighs together. I have never been more turned on in my entire life.

"You will have to teach me how you like to be pleased," I say to him, allowing myself to drown in his eyes— a mind-numbing high that is far beyond explanation. "Teach me to please you."

"You may not remember but you like sucking my cocks. I do not have to teach you anything. Once you have me in your mouth, you will remember, trust me."

I tremble as Aldrick's coarse hair drags deli- ciously across my skin, each strand a tiny whip of sensation that intensifies his scent. His masculine musk invades my nostrils and is like a lightning bolt to my senses. With a grip of iron, he coaxes me even closer, and I find myself lost in an ocean of pleasure as I explore the expanse of his body. His taste and smell are overwhelming, and it feels like he has no boundaries so I can submerge myself in his deli- ciousness.

I wrap my hand around the base of his larger shaft. In close view, I am even more impressed by this tool than ever. It is enormous—worryingly so and startlingly thick with a rosy, pink tip that is flushed with arousal. I stroke it slowly as I wet my lips. It is a strange feeling to want something so much and be afraid of it at the same damn time.

"Fuck, Jane, you're driving me crazy," he growls.

I am pumped with a sense of power. Earlier, he had implied that he would like it if I stood up to him and now, I am easily complying with his every demand. A mischievous thought enters my head: could I use this as an opportunity to unsettle him and make him squirm in raw desire? Could I put him into the same state of vulnerability that he has made me experience?

I stroke him with a feather light touch—once, twice—then lean forward and press my lips against his shaft. So hot, so decadent. The taste of sugar explodes on my tongue and I close my eyes to savor the flavor. But it isn't enough. I want more. With a sudden burst of courage, I drag my tongue along him and bite back a proud smirk when I hear him moan with pleasure, then release a loud groan. I trace circles with my tongue around his tip and feel the quaking of his legs beneath me as he shudders in delight. I look up at him then and let loose a wicked smile of satisfaction because this is all because of me —no matter how small a victory it might be.

"I do have a few tricks up my sleeve," I whisper, letting him know he's not the only one who can drive us wild with desire.

Aldrick only lets me play with him for so long. A hard and heavy hand on the back of my head presses me forward and urges me to take him deep into my mouth. I wrap my lips around him, opening my mouth wide and licking him at the same time. With just a small part of him in my mouth, a deep hunger takes over me to take in all of him. I want him deep down in my throat, filling me up with his massive cock and seed. But I am smart enough to know I am not ready for that just yet.

I swirl my tongue around him, affording myself the time and space to get used to the taste, size, and feeling. When my tongue passes over the tip, a sweet-salty taste hits my mouth that makes me wild and greedy for more. This man's cock is addicting and I could suck it my whole life. Aldrick keeps his eyes on me as I work his shaft, his glowing eyes unblinking. That cocky smirk also never leaves his face, giving his attractiveness a devilish side that pulls me in.

"You are such a tease, Jane," he says to me. "You keep playing with my cock like that and you will not know what hits you when the breeding begins."

There is something in Aldrick's voice that always sets off a dose of unholy lust in me. The moment he mentions breeding me, I am energized and begin to slide down on him, taking deep breaths as more and more of his lengthy shaft enters my mouth. My jaw starts to ache because he is huge and I am struggling, but I love the control I have over him.

"Easy, girl," Aldrick grunts. "Careful or you might injure yourself."

I am not inclined to listen to him. I just keep bopping down his cock, determined to show him the brightest stars and whitest skies he has ever seen. But despite my enthusiasm, I can only take him so far because then I start to gag.

Aldrick bellows out a deafening roar, so loud I'm certain it could shatter every window in the room. My body tenses as I take in the sight of him. His knees buckle and his cocks quiver violently, the silvery shafts glowing brightly under the light of the lamps.

My eyes widen as I take in the sheer size of the two cocks in my hands, one in each. My mouth waters uncontrollably and I slip the first manhood between my lips without hesitation, feeling it slide like silk against my tongue. The pleasure that blankets me is incomparable, and I can hardly contain myself as I wrap my right hand around the other cock while I continue to savor the delectable taste of the first. An insatiable desire begins to simmer within me as I imagine taking them both at once. As I suck them off, juice pools in copious amounts between my legs.

When I look up at him, there is a darkness in his glowing eyes and I start to wonder if I should I be doing this when everything so far seems to work against us? There is my impaired trust for him, then also his sister, who's determined to get rid of me to make way for her own machinations. Should I not make sure that things are normal and settled before getting in bed with Aldrick? Perhaps I should, but who can blame me? Is there anyone in the world who would be able to resist this sexy beast?

With one hand under my chin, he guides me forward again. "You can take more of me, Jane," he says.

If I could speak, I might have argued but with his cock completely filling my mouth and his strong hand at the back of my head keeping me steady, there is no way I can utter a single word and quite frankly, I don't want to. "You're doing so well. I bet your pussy is soaking for me," he says.

You bet.

I moan in response, my eyes streaming with tears as his cock hits the back of my throat. But my enthusiasm does not reduce the size of his cock or increase the size of my mouth. I try to take him all in, but my jaw is aching so much, I pull away for a moment to take a deep breath. "You've done this before," he says, massaging my scalp gently. "But don't worry. I'll help you."

Aldrick grabs my chin with an iron grip and harshly pulls me closer, thrusting his cock deeper into my mouth and groaning loudly. I gasp for breath as he fills me up, taking me to a place of euphoria I never knew existed. My thoughts spiral out of control with every push, yet I want more, begging him to never let go.

"Do you want me to fuck your mouth, Jane," he asks even though he is already doing that. "Do you think you could handle that?"

At this point there is no going back so I nod. He fists my hair, drawing my head back with a strong pull to make me look at him. His cock pops out of my mouth, then he gently rubs my cheek, giving me one minute of tenderness within all this fiery passion. "If this starts to become more than you can bear, just sink your teeth into my cock and I will stop immediately," he instructs.

In response, I nod vigorously. "Yes, Aldrick, yes ... I understand."

"Good girl, choke on that dick. You're mine to do with as I please."

I don't know why but his crude words are making me wetter, needier.

Keeping my head steady between his hands, he uses his thumbs to spread my mouth wide open and I relax my jaw to the best of my ability. He presses his cock back into me, the tip touching my tongue first and then the shaft filling me up.

When it hits the back of my throat, I take in deep breaths and relax, ignoring the way he's assaulting my mouth, letting him push and push while focusing on the sounds that escape his lips. My pussy throbs with every inch of his cock I'm able to take, every groan he emits, and my right hand travels between my thighs so I can pleasure myself as I pleasure him.

I take in almost his entire length, but he does what I am not able to, moving me along his cock as he fucks my mouth. He quickly picks up the pace as I gag on his shaft, fucking me mercilessly. I mirror his actions by rubbing myself with the intensity of his movement. Waves of pleasure crest over me multiple times in moments, and I fear I might go blind. Aldrick growls something and it seems like he might release his seed in my mouth, but with one powerful motion, he pulls me off his dick and takes one step back from me.

His breathing rugged, he dangles his huge cocks right in front of my face, then lifts me up off my knees to push me on the bed, coming to hover above me. I whimper when his mouth roughly devours mine. Then he pinches my left nipple unexpectedly, and I draw in a sharp breath. "Oh, Aldrick," I moan into his mouth, wriggling underneath him.

He hungrily licks and bites my skin, tracing a wild path down my body with his tongue. His hands move like lightning, more animal than human as he rips my undergarments away. When his eyes meet mine it feels like the air has been sucked from the room and I know in that very moment, I belong to him.

"You are mine now, Jane," he growls. "Say it."

"I am yours," I hear myself say. "Take me."

His tongue moves over my soaking slit and I tremble, needing more as he grips my ass cheeks. I tug hard on his horns while he buries his face into my throbbing pussy and starts licking it furiously. Liquid heat spreads through my veins.

Aldrick spreads my legs wider then slides his surprisingly long tongue into me and starts fucking me with it. Loud and unbridled screams of pleasure leave my lips. The air is charged with desire and his strong energy—the thought of the entire castle hearing us sounds so enticing. I'm so close to exploding, but I need him inside me and he must be sensing it too because he stops and lifts his head.

Just as I am about to ask him to keep going, Aldrick presses a thick finger into me and draws a sharp breath. There is absolutely nothing soft about this invasion. It is rough and I like it.

"Look at you, Jane," he says as he fucks me hard with his finger. "You like it rough, don't you, little one?"

He pulls his finger from inside me then I watch in awe as he puts his fingers in his mouth, licking all my pussy juices with unbridled joy. I want to say something but whatever it is that comes to my mind turns into mush when he returns his mouth to me again. Naturally, I try to pull back because this kind of pleasure is just too much for a mere mortal like me to receive at once, but I am unable to move an inch.

With his hands on my hips, holding me down, he devours me, feasting on my pussy like the monster he truly is. His tongue keeps on moving and I arch my back in abandon. I moan his name, pleading him to make me orgasm, but my voice comes out muffled and incoherent. Aldrick is driving me to the edge. My thighs begin to tremble as he sucks on my clit until I see black dots in my vision. My pussy aches with the need for release and I am so close—just one lick and I'd be there.

"You cannot come, Jane. Not yet," he says.

"Why?" I ask desperately, so wet and so close...

"Because the breeding hasn't even begun." He rises from between my thighs and hovers over me.

Aldrick's fingers slide up my ribs and brush over my nipple, and it feels so good with his big body pressing into me that I close my eyes.

"Open your eyes, Jane," he says, his voice commanding. "I want you to know who is fucking you."

When I do what he asks, Aldrick's his giant cock nudges my entrance. Then he thrusts into me and I scream as he fills me with his length. My hands fly around him as he moves in and out, hard and fast. I throw my head back and my eyes roll upward, a scream ensuing as he hits my G-spot. My breaths come out in shallow gasps. I am powerless to his touch, unable to catch my breath or form a coherent thought, let alone find the strength to tell him to keep fucking me. But Aldrick does not need encouragement, he senses my helplessness and ravages me without hesitation.

The orgasm shatters through me, pleasure fills my veins and I cry out as he keeps fucking me savagely. After caressing my stomach, he roughly cups my breasts, squeezing both hard. He takes me mercilessly and touches me in ways that drive me to insanity.

"This isn't over, Jane," he groans as he stills for a moment. "We are not near the end yet and I must also fill you with my second cock."

Panting, I cannot find the strength to speak or even move. Did he just say that he's going to double penetrate me? I don't think I am ready for whatever he has planned for us, but a split second later, Aldrick gets back into action. He flips me over on my knees again and buries himself deeper inside me. Then, I gasp when his second cock nudges the entrance to my ass. I have never been fucked there and I'm not sure I could take it. Both of his cocks are huge.

"Just relax, Jane," he says as he feels my body

tensing. "I need to fuck you with both of my cocks. Trust me, you will love it. This is the only way to get my seed. The only way for this to come to completion."

"Yes," I finally say, wanting and needing more of him. "Breed me. Spill your precious seed inside me."

Aldrick growls in approval then slowly pushing his second cock into my asshole as he rubs my clit with his hand. This feels more pleasant than I expected. My body screams with pleasure as my soul is pulled between Heaven and Hell. Aldrick's two powerful cocks thrust deep within me, one pounding into my pussy and the other in my ass, sending waves of immense pleasure cascading through me.

I look over my shoulder to see his eyes are alight with the rapture that engulfs us both. He bends down toward me, kissing my temple as he moves inside me with a special gentility. Making love to me with two cocks at the same time, he slides in and out of both my holes like he owns them ... and he does. He rests his head against my nape while I scream incoherently. I'm so utterly gone now. I want so much and Aldrick gives it all to me without me needing to ask.

When I feel Aldrick's teeth sink into my neck, I

know he is close. In one movement, I reach behind me and grab his tail, stroking it as he keeps pounding into me. I come apart, seeing stars, then he screams my name as he comes inside me.

His seed gushes into me like a tidal wave, seeming to never end. I feel as if I'm being overcome by it and consumed until he finally pulls out. When I turn, I witness an explosion of glitter and stars bursting forth from his member, illuminating the room in a dazzling array of color that almost makes my senses go numb. A sight unlike anything I had ever seen before.

Soon, he is as spent as I am and I lie down so he falls on top of me. I don't even complain about the possibility that he might crush me. This monster is a god and it does not get better than this.

CHAPTER
TWELVE

For several hours after my encounter with Aldrick, I stay in my room and refuse to leave. This is simply because I do not know how to deal with what Aldrick and I did and the possibility of having Lena or Karken find out. If they found out we had slept together, their laughter would burn my ears as they'd call me a massive hypocrite. And I can only imagine Lena's rage upon learning that Aldrick and I have become allies again —which is exactly the opposite of what she wants.

When Herb, Knox, and Teon come to fetch me for dinner, I refuse to go, insisting that they bring the food to me after I lie to them that I don't feel too well. This gives them a good enough reason not to push me further or ask any more questions. Aldrick must realize how I feel because he doesn't come to my room to check if everything is all right. He most likely understands why I might not want to engage with his guests after he fucked my brains out earlier on. I suspect Karken might smell his scent all over me if I show up for dinner.

Throughout the night, I am unable to sleep for extended periods. Every hour or two, I am awakened by a bad dream, all of which are similar to one another: Aldrick and I are in the middle of an activity such as walking around the garden, reading, or doing indecent things to each other when we are suddenly being dragged away by other monsters that attack the castle.

As the clock inches closer to midnight, I make a conscious decision to stay awake. My eyes grow heavy and my limbs tired, but I fear going to sleep—fear the nightmares that would follow if I do. So I stay awake, fighting my exhaustion until finally I grant myself a few hours of rest, free from the haunting of the monster siblings in all their unwelcome glory.

My heart races when I wake up in the morning, knowing that I cannot make excuses this time. Herb, Knox, and Teon will soon be here to take me to the garden so I can have my morning bath. What lies ahead is a minefield of questions that must be answered with care—how am I going to face Karken, Khimaira, or Lena without giving away my inner turmoil?

Unfortunately, I don't have enough time to prepare myself to face the monsters in the castle because just as I am pacing around the room, thinking of what I can do, the door opens and all three servants arrive.

"Hello, Jane," Herb says. "It's time for your morning bath. We are hoping you're feeling much better this morning?"

"Yes I am well rested. In fact, I think I will enjoy this bath tremendously."

With my memories flooding back more and more, I am beginning to recall the days I spent in this castle weeks ago. I feel my heart quickening as I remember all the fun and laughter I shared with Aldrick, but even more intense was Herb, Teon, and Knox's presence that was always around us. With this new knowledge, I look upon them with a newfound appreciation and admiration.

Watching them now as they walk in front of me in the dimly lit hallway with their big cocks swinging between their legs, wild fantasies unfold in my mind. Will this castle ever be sane and have just five of us again so we can have those moments back? Once Aldrick siblings leave then this might be my new reality. It seems the monster's servants have actively participated in our intimate moments in the past, and he doesn't mind sharing me with them.

As we enter the garden, I hear voices and my first instinct is to return to my room but I tell myself I'm ready to face any challenges they throw at me. I have nowhere to run to anyway because Herb and Teon are standing on either side of me. They are loyal to Aldrick and are here to serve him, so I don't want to get them into any trouble, especially now after I remember the way they always took care of me.

I proceed begrudgingly to the pool and the voices get louder. I hope it's Aldrick is greeting some other guests that have unexpectedly shown up so I don't have to deal with Lena, Karken, and Khimaira.

"Well, well, well, if it isn't the human princess," Lena says in a mocking tone. She is lying on the grass under a tree to my right, with a book in front of her.

I hate the bitch and don't even feel bad about it.

I refuse to be drawn in by her juvenile taunts so I keep trudging forward, my gaze fixated on the pool just ahead where Karken and Khimaira are joyfully horsing around. My stony silence only serves to amplify Lena's anger until it bubbles up and bursts forth, and before I know it she is blocking my path, her eyes alive with fury.

"I'm surprised you are still here," she says with a mocking smile. I'm shaking with anger, ready to punch her, but I can't give her the satisfaction she craves. "Tell me, Jane, isn't it true that you want to leave but aren't able to just walk away? Despite your denial, you must know now that you are nothing but a prisoner here."

"You don't have to do this, Lena," I say, aware of her biting words. My jaw clenches and my fists curl in anger, yet no words escape my lips as I battle for control over my emotions.

"Oh, but I do," she says. Khimaira laughs in the pool behind us when Karken lifts her by the waist and throws her back in the water, causing a big splash. Those two are in a special world of their own. I cannot help but wonder what it would take to have that or even better with Aldrick ... such a preferable state to fighting with Lena. "I will not stand by and let an imposter traipse around this castle like she owns it."

I want to turn around and walk away but I still have a little fire in me that is enough to stand my ground. "I just want to have my bath. Have a great day, Lena," I say with the best smile I can muster, then make to move past her.

A searing pain shoots up my arm when Lena grabs a hold of me and prevents me from walking away. I release a loud yelp which is enough to grab the attention of the lovers in the pool and stop all their splashing.

"Unhand her," Herb says, now beside me. His brothers join us, menacing expressions on their faces.

"You will stay out of this if you don't want to lose your heads," Lena spats, each word laced with venom. "Don't forget that you are nothing but servants."

"Let me go, Lena!" I yell at her, but her grip grows tighter. I should fight back but a feeling of helplessness keeps me rooted in place, enduring her malicious torture.

"Listen to me very carefully. In a few hours..." she starts to say but Karken is already out of the pool and he doesn't look happy.

"Hey!" Karken shouts, walking toward us completely naked. I try to look away but his two huge cocks are hard to miss. "Let her go."

"Stay out of this, Karken," she barks without looking back at him. "This is none of your business."

"Let. Her. Go. Lena," he repeats, enunciating every word and closing in on us. "Jane belongs to Aldrick and I won't let you hurt her."

Lena finally lets me go by my pushing me away and stepping back. "Fine," she says, putting her hands up in surrender. "Everybody comes to the rescue of the human princess."

Karken inserts himself in the space between us. He is facing his sister, so I can't read him at all, but it is noble of him to stand up to her for me. It's not like I expected this from him.

"Don't be a fool, Lena," he says to her.

His sister hisses like a venomous snake. "You're going to regret this," she warns. Luckily, Karken's frame separates me from Lena's wrath. She is determined to make me suffer.

"Jane has done nothing wrong. She's Aldrick's mate through and through. I can see it now," Karken speaks with great emphasis.

For a few moments, Lena says nothing. Then she suddenly moves, lifting her chin so we can see each other past the wall of Karken's shoulders, her lips stretching into the devilish smirk I'm all too familiar with. "Take a good look around," she speaks in a low voice full of spite and malicious intent. "This might be the last time you get to enjoy this garden."

As she walks away, her stiletto heels click against the ground like a ticking time bomb. My heart pounds as I watch her leave, and I feel like a coward for not speaking up with more strength. Karken's gaze follows her out the door with a wicked glint, as though he relishes her discomfort. He does not look sympathetic or even remotely bothered by the interaction. In fact, he looks like he enjoyed it. Sometimes, Aldrick's brother is very difficult to read.

"Thank you," I say to him.

"I wouldn't worry about Lena," Karken says. "She's all bark and no bite."

He starts to walk toward the pool which Khimaira has also stepped out of and is now drying herself next to it.

"I don't like to see that side of her. What did she mean by saying that this would be my last time in the garden?" A thousand questions sit on the tip of my tongue. Every second feels like an eternity as he ponders his answer.

He takes in a deep breath as we stop beside Khimaira. He puts his left arm around her and pulls her closer to him, his face more serious than I have ever seen him be. "I am not so sure but if I know Lena, she has a plan which might unravel anytime from now. Don't worry, I will keep her out of your way like I promised."

"Is she going to kill me?" I ask.

Karken smiles in response and for the first time since I have met him, it appears to be a genuine smile. "She won't kill you. She hasn't got the guts for it. Besides, Aldrick would not let her, especially not after the heaven you showed him in his chambers yesterday."

I stare at him in disbelief. Has he been spying on us? The reactions of those around us tell me that he has made an unexpected revelation. Khimaira wears an expression of shock, followed by the beginnings of a smile. Herb, Teon, and Knox all seem stunned at first, but soon they are beaming with happiness, as if they have been waiting for this news all along.

"How did you know?" I ask, my cheeks on fire. "Did Aldrick tell you?"

"These castle walls have ears and your mate does not moan at low volumes," he says with a shrug and my face is ablaze. Then his gaze darts behind me. "Speak of the devil and he appears."

My heart races as I catch Aldrick walking towards us, his eyes narrowing with suspicion. Memories of our fervent lovemaking take all the space in my mind and it is the hardest thing to act normal. He closes in on me, while Karken and Khimaira stay put like silent spectators, watching us with bated breath.

"Jane," he says, and I melt. He caresses my cheek then trails his hand to my shoulder, where he begins to trace my exposed clavicle with his finger. He leans down to my ear. "I'd hoped you didn't have a chance to have your bath yet. I need to breathe you in."

"Oh," is all I manage to say.

Aldrick takes my arm and pulls me toward the pool. His gaze is focused solely on me, ignoring everyone around us. He strips off my clothes with a steady determination, baring my body without so much as a word passing between us.

"Aldrick," I say gently, grabbing his wrist before my dress falls off my body. "Your brother and his mate are here. Your servants are here."

Aldrick smiles. "Last night I filled you with my seed and I am certain that you are with child. I only want us to feel each other like we did yesterday. Nothing can stop me, not even their presence. Let Karken and Khimaira watch if they want to. It's time for us to return the favor they've given us way too many times. And as for my servants,' he says, looking at Herb, Teon, and Knox who are standing beside us expectantly, "just invite them and they'll join. They are here to please you. We all are."

I feel a little apprehensive about this whole situation, but I'm getting more turned on knowing that everyone will watch us fucking. Suddenly, this doesn't feel strange anymore. My dress slips from my body, falling like a waterfall to the floor in a heap. Aldrick moves with such swiftness that I don't have time to register what's happening before my skin is bare. His own clothes follow just as quickly, revealing his strong physique and making me ache for him as always. Then he reaches for me, our raw hunger for each other palpable in the atmosphere. He lifts me off my feet, effortlessly maneuvering me into the pool of water where he slowly lowers me until we are both submerged in a tight embrace.

"Hold on," I say coyly, feeling bold. "Maybe your servants should prime me for you with their cocks?"

Aldrick nods in agreement and quickly retreats, pressing his back against the far wall of the pool. His servants step into the water and creep toward me like sharks in the open sea. Meanwhile, I catch a glimpse of Karken and Khimaira watching us intently, their faces beaming with pleasure. Their passion excites me beyond reason and I'm left feeling empowered by their presence. It has become clear that this is normal custom in Moorhead—being shared and cherished. Maybe these creatures have had it right all along.

The servant brothers hold the soap firmly in their hands, slowly and deliberately lathering every inch of my body. Nothing is left untouched as they sensually rub the soap over my curves, taking their time to ensure that I am clean and refreshed. Their touch lingers on me like a kiss, leaving me feeling aroused and alive.

An undeniable hunger radiates from their eyes. They take me in, their minuscule bodies visibly aching to wrap around me, impale me on their giant cocks. When my gaze settles on Herb, I'm met with pure carnal desire, as if his entire being is focused solely on me. My body hums in response and anticipation reigns as my fingers trail delicately over my nipple. His breath falters and his cock twitches at the sight of me, but he valiantly tamps down his arousal.

He trails his hand gently down my rib cage until it settles between my thighs, exploring me with a deftness that sets my whole body alight. His touch is electric as he parts my legs like an open book, unleashing a wave of pleasure through me. Teon and Knox join us, taking each of my breasts in their hands and driving me closer to rapture with their touch. All the while, Aldrick watches, his ripped body ready to join in the ecstasy of our ultimate union.

Herb nudges my entrance with his cock as if asking for permission to enter me so when he rubs my clit, I let out a moan of approval. Moments later, he stops touching me with his hands and discards the soap to push his big cock almost all the way in.

He moves torturously slow but finally thrusts his shaft into me. I scramble for something to anchor myself on, but all my hands can find is the slimy edge of the pool. Aldrick appears behind me in that moment, his strong arms clamping around my waist to pin me in place while his servants ravish my body with their passionate touches, bites, and licks while Karken and Khimaira watch, enthralled, and shamelessly explore each other.

Herb assaults me with unbridled passion, diving hard and fast into me, his hands digging into my flesh while the other two servants squeeze and pinch my nipples. Pleasure swells within me, triggering a chorus of whimpers and moans. Aldrick silences me by moving to my side, where Teon was standing, shoving one of his cocks down my throat. Just like that, he sucks me into a realm of unimaginable delight. My entire body quakes in anticipation of the heavenly bliss that awaits.

I to figure out who it is, Knox or Teon, that now stands behind me, holding me steady. Before I am given time to decide, Herb dives underwater and starts rubbing my asshole, slowly easing his fingers in while his brother fucks me from behind like a maniac. This is all too much and I'm beginning to lose my mind. Every inch of my body trembles as I'm just about to explode, my senses heightened to breaking point.

As if on cue, Knox climbs out of the pool and joins Karken and his mate. Karken thrusts deeply into Khimaira while Knox circles around her and thrusts his giant cock into her mouth—as Aldrick is doing to me. For a long moment all I can hear are the loud moans and sounds of fucking. The sensual, erotic sounds fill me with delight, leading me toward a soul-shattering orgasm.

I scream, my voice met with an echoing chorus from Khimaira in a rousing call-and-response pattern of pure pleasure. The intensity of our cries electrifies me and speeds up my journey to the brink. The climax rips through me—once, twice, and then again and again as Teon keeps pounding into me from behind and while Herb fingers my butthole.

Every nerve in my body ignites with awareness as Aldrick simultaneously ravishes my mouth, triggering a white-hot explosion that surges throughout my body yet another time. As his seed spills into my throat, I'm left gasping for air and trembling from the violence of it all.

When I finally open my eyes, everyone is watching me. I let out a deep sigh of blissful exhaustion before sinking into the pool of warm water which blankets me like a soothing balm.

THIRTEEN

My heart pounds in my chest as I approach the meeting hall. A sense of dread fills me, even though there should be nothing to worry about. My sixth sense screams at me that something is off. Aldrick and I are supposed to discuss our mating rules, but my excitement has turned to fear. When Herb told me that Aldrick was ready for me, I imagined a passionate union, not this creeping terror. With each step closer to the door of the meeting hall, my anxiety grows until it becomes an overwhelming force threatening to consume me entirely.

I reach the door, an invisible force causing me to recoil from the voices that bellow from inside. Instinctively, I want to flee and never look back, but

Aldrick has risked so much to get here that turning away now would be tantamount to betrayal. Steeling my resolve, I push open the door and take a step into the fray. The arguing within is deafening, each voice louder than the last, filled with vitriol and spite.

"There she is!" Lena's voice lands in my ears like a heap of shards tossed at me. From the way she turns to face me from the end of the room, it is clear she has been waiting for my arrival just so she can make a scene out of it. "The thorn in everyone's flesh. The rash that refuses to go away."

"Lena, shut up. You're crossing the line right now," Aldrick snaps at her, leaving her side and coming to meet me in the middle of the room.

"What's going on?" I whisper as he pulls me closer to him. We stand together while everybody else watches on.

"There is a little problem but I will handle it," he says before leaving me to face the rest of the room.

"Oh please, I have done this for your own good, big brother, and you'll thank me for it one day," Lena declares dramatically.

I stare at them and then glance around while wondering why they haven't called me sooner so I'm up to speed with what's going on. Then I notice another person I have never seen before. It's a woman and who is definitely from Moorhead. I can tell from the way she's dressed and her similar build to Lena. Besides, she has horns.

The woman is staring directly at me, a tentative smile on her lips. Unlike Lena who has jet black hair, she has copper red hair and is—I admit—incredibly attractive. Despite her beauty, I feel justified in instantly hating her because she must be the replacement mate Aldrick's sister found for him. She is adamant on raising hell and convincing their people a human female is an unacceptable match. If Aldrick seals his union with me, he'd be betraying his own.

I go to take Aldrick's hand and bring him closer to me.

"Just calm down, dearest" I tell him, gripping his cheeks with white-knuckled fingers, trying desperately to push my words of comfort into him. "We will find a way to be together. Our bond is too strong for her to break. If we stand together, she will never win."

But my efforts are in vain for resentment blazes in Aldrick's eyes. Not that I can blame him. The game Lena is playing is a dangerous one indeed, ultimately risking great divisions and possibly even war.

"My sister has gone too far this time, Jane. We can't just sit back and watch, letting her take away what we hold most dear," he says through the gritted teeth.

"What?" I ask, panic brewing in me with every passing second. "What has she done?"

"Wouldn't you like to know?" Lena says, her voice dripping with mockery.

Aldrick springs from my grasp in a single, powerful movement, and before I can fathom his intentions, his hands are wrapped around Lena's throat. He slams her against the wall with such force that all of the paintings hanging on it shake violently and come crashing to the floor. Everyone takes a step back—all but Karken, who sprints forward to try and separate his brother and sister.

"What did she do?" I ask. "Please don't hurt her."

"You need to stay out of their way," Khimaira says, grabbing my hand that I instantly try yank away. They cannot be serious. Aldrick is not going to hurt his sister. This is insane.

"Please, Jane," Herb says, appearing out of

SOPHIA SMUT

nowhere. "Master Aldrick will deal with his sister accordingly. You cannot get involved."

I am powerless against the forces around me. As I watch helplessly, Lena's face morphs into a twisted mask of pleasure as someone twice her size pins her against the wall and begins to choke her. I can see the mad grin tugging at her lips, as if she relishes in her own captivity and takes delight in asserting her dominance over me. Though I'm still perplexed by the situation, it is clear that Lena has already won.

"What did she do?" I ask Khimaira, the panic I am feeling now showing in my trembling voice.

"Prevented Aldrick from mating with you," Khimaira explains, and I want to scream.

"How did she do it?" I ask. "Please, just tell me. I have to know."

"I took your only claim to be Aldrick's mate!" Lena screams out, loud enough for me to hear.

"Shut your mouth!" Aldrick yells at her, pushing her further into the wall so that she shows the first sign of actually being hurt in the way her eyes snap shut.

"What is she talking about?" I am more confused than ever.

"There is a potion that you are supposed to take so you will be able to bear Aldrick's child," Karken

168

says as Lena struggles to free herself from Aldrick's hold. "Without it, you will die if you get pregnant. The baby will tear you apart from the inside. She has taken it and given it to that peppermint over there."

"My name is Sara," the redhead says, stepping forward. "And yes, I have taken the potion."

The crushing weight of the situation lands on me like a sledgehammer to the chest. So she did not only question Aldrick's authority in front of his family and people. She schemed to physically and emotionally inflict harm on us. Fury takes over common sense as I realize Aldrick's true feelings, and how easily she has manipulated both me and my future child for her own twisted desires. Her evil actions have condemned me to death—if I don't get that potion, I'll surely perish with my child.

I confront Aldrick, demanding an answer to her deceit.

"Why didn't you tell me about this potion?!" I ask him, barely containing my rage.

"Because I never thought Lena would do such a thing!" he roars. All of his rage is directed at Lena who he chokes even harder.

"Just let her go, please," Karken says, tugging on Aldrick's arms until he releases her. She falls into a fit of coughs, holding her throat, but the smug smile never leaves her face.

"You will never get away with this," Aldrick says to her.

"Are you going to kill me? Your own sister?" she mocks him. From the look of Aldrick, he's actually considering it, but Karken is doing his job to restrain him. Her smile widens. "Good. Now that we have that settled and the human distraction knows her place, I suggest that you take Sara up to your chambers and fuck her like you mean it. Unlike that weakling, she will be able to carry your child and give you what you deserve."

My heart is about to burst out of my chest and shatter in a million pieces. I want to scream or move but Khimaira's grip on my hand is like iron, trapping me between her and Herb. Anxiety cripples me and all I can do is stand there, powerless.

"Herb, lead Sara to Aldrick's chambers and prepare her for him," Lena says condescendingly.

"My prince, I'll be waiting for you," Sara says seductively to Aldrick, then begins to walk away. He hesitates and I see how painful this is for him. It is a bitch to contain my infinite anger and disappointment. Aldrick has no choice and now I regret that I didn't leave earlier when I had a chance. I don't think my poor heart will ever heal if I leave Moorhead.

"Okay, stop!" Karken says suddenly. "Aldrick shouldn't be with this woman because Jane is his true mate. Where did you find her, Lena?"

"It doesn't matter," Lena says. "And there is nothing you can do about it. I wish you would all see that I am doing this for all our sakes. We cannot allow a human into this castle to have the power that comes with being Aldrick's mate. She would be able to destroy us all with a snap of her fingers."

"You're doing this just so you can have some control over me?" Aldrick asks, shaking his head in disbelief.

"If that is how you wish to see it, fine," she says with a shrug. "It is too late anyway."

"I don't think so," Karken says, sporting his own special version of a wicked smile. "You forget just how much I know you, Lena."

"And you think too much of yourself, Karken," she spits out.

"Perhaps. But I have a little surprise for you."

Karken snakes his hand out of his pocket, clutching a small cylindrical container. His smile grows like wildfire, while Lena's face drains of color and Aldrick stands rigidly with clenched fists. The tension in the air thickens when Karken holds up the mysterious object, almost daring them to believe what it contains.

"What is that?" Aldrick asks.

"This is your potion," Karken says proudly. "I suspected that she might do something this stupid when Jane confided her thoughts to me. I knew that Aldrick would not get rid of Jane no matter what Lena says so she would have to resort to some dirty games such as this. While you two were busy fucking each other's brains out, I came here and switched the potion vial with water, transferring the real thing to this little container here, just in case."

"What?" Lena shrieks in horror but Karken is unfazed by her outburst. He turns to face Sara with the smile still plastered on his face. The woman has not left yet, no doubt drawn by the intense exchange.

Revulsion and dread register on both Sara and Lena's faces as they gasp in both horror and disgust. Their eyes are like fiery volcanoes about to erupt. Lena lunges toward Karken like a missile. Yet the man stands unflinching, his grip on her wrist so strong, she grimaces in pain. As their eyes meet, it's clear that whatever strength she possesses is nothing compared to this man's.

"Stop embarrassing yourself, Lena," he says. "You've lost like you always have."

Lena recoils from his touch as though she was struck by lightning, her features twisted in a mask of displeasure. She carefully edges away from him and gives Aldrick an expression filled with sorrow and regret, every emotion etched into her face as clear as day. She wordlessly for a second chance, one that he may grant her but with a heavy heart.

"Aldrick, my brother, I only did this because I care for you. You must remember what those humans have done to our family. I was looking out for you. I'm so sorry," she says, tugging at his arms as crocodile tears fall from her eyes. She is excellent at playing the role of the victim.

Aldrick says nothing as his sister pleads, her voice quivering with desperation. She sinks to her knees, hands clasped tightly together in a desperate attempt to beg for mercy. In an unexpected move, she whips around and launches an accusing finger at Sara, eyes blazing and throat hoarse from pleading.

"It was her. She tricked me. She threatened me. She made me do it because she wants you so bad."

"No!" Sara says fearfully. "You were the one who convinced me to do this. You assured me!"

"Stop this, Lena," Aldrick says, sounding bored. "You've done enough."

Lena rises slowly from the floor, swallowing the rest of her tears and taking a deep breath. "Fine," she says, wiping her face. "But I still have one act left in me."

My heart races as Lena whips around fixes her hateful gaze on me. I stand frozen, my feet heavy as lead as I catch sight of a glint of metal sticking out from her dress. In an instant, she pulls out a blade, the razor edge dripping with menace. With predatory grace and a whole lot of madness, she lunges towards me.

Everything happens too fast. Time stands still as Khimaira dives towards me, yanking my body out of harm's way. Karken and Herb propel themselves in Lena's direction while I'm thrown to the ground like a ragdoll. I can barely make sense of what is going on when I finally raise my head and catch Aldrick's leer, his fingers entwined in Lena's hair, holding her own dagger against her throat.

"Now you've *really* gone too far," he says, then pushes her violently. She hits the floor like a sack of potatoes and whimpers. She scrambles to get up again but Aldrick walks toward her shouts at her to stay down. Bending down to her level, he looks straight into her eyes, his expression unreadable. "Listen to me carefully. Jane is my mate and you have made a terrible mistake in plotting against her. I have half a mind to kill you for all you have done but I cannot find it in myself to do that. Now, I want you to look around because this is the last time you will ever be welcome in this castle."

"No!" she cries.

"You are banished from this castle and my territory for life," he says, shocking everyone, including Karken, who looks like he is enjoying this entire scene a little too much. "If you come anywhere close, I will kill you. I give you twenty minutes to pack your things and leave, never to return."

Lena bolts upright and sprints out of the hall without a backward glance. Sara scurries in her wake, her gaze darting from side to side as she desperately calls out for Lena to wait. The great hall is overcome by silence, punctured only by the two women's frenzied panting and Sara's desolate pleas.

"Karken," Aldrick says, turning toward his brother. "What you did was phenomenal."

"And..." Karken responds jokingly.

"And what?"

"You're not going to thank me for saving you and

your mate?" Karken teases. "This is why nobody likes you."

Aldrick chuckles at that and grabs his brother's shoulder. "Thank you," he says. Finally, he turns toward me and closes the distance between us. He places his hands on either side of my waist and holds me. My stomach flutters. "I'm sorry for what my sister has put you through."

"It's okay," I respond with a smile. "You were also a target."

"Now we can finally live in this castle as we are supposed to."

"Yes," I sigh. "Yes, we can."

Aldrick cups my chin and pulls me up to him until our faces are mere inches apart. He leans in and brushes his lips over mine with a fire that licks every inch of my being. His kiss deepens with a hunger that leaves us both breathless as we cling to each other. The world around us dissolves into nothing but our own desire as we explore each other with a newfound intensity.

I break the kiss to whisper in his ear, "I love you. You're *mine*, Aldrick, and always will be."

I may be his to possess, but this monster of Mount Moorhead also belongs to me.

DOROTHY'S POV

I knock on Jane's door, louder this time. Maybe she is sleeping inside and just did not hear me knock the first time. I call her name, but she still doesn't respond. Every second that passes is another step further down the rabbit hole as far as I'm concerned. She has been making so much effort to adjust to life ever since her hike up the mountain, but I feel like she's just one wrong decision away from plunging back into depression. The memory of finding her in a pile on the floor while her bedroom blazed around her months ago still haunts me, leaving me with an unbearable fear of the same fate repeating itself.

"Jane!" I call out to no response. "Are you in there? Open up."

My heart hammers in my chest as I put my hand on the door to Jane's apartment. Scouring my memory bank for any hint as to where she might be, I remember the spare key hidden at the top of her doorframe. I reach up, sliding my fingers around the frame, until I come in contact with the cold metal. With a trembling hand, I insert the key into the lock and open the door, desperately hoping there will be an answer inside that will tell me where Jane has gone.

"Hello?" I walk in, willing Jane to walk out and say she has been sleeping or something. "Where the hell are you?"

I frantically pull my phone from my pocket, my hands trembling as I dial Jane yet again. With each unanswered ring my stomach clenches with worry and dread. I can see her phone glowing on the coffee table, but without her there it's like a dying ember in an abandoned fireplace—a clear signal that some-thing is wrong. Every ounce of me knows something isn't right and as this nightmare fills my soul, I'm left to wonder where my best friend could possibly be.

I rush around the apartment, tearing open doors, desperate for any sign of her. My heart is in my throat as I search each room, each closet, and no relief comes when I am finished. Fuck! Where could she be? If her phone is here then she can't be far away—but nobody in town has seen her! Could someone have taken her? My mind races with the terrifying possibilities.

I rush to the kitchen counter, hands trembling. My eyes fixate on a single piece of paper and I snatch it off the countertop. The writing is unmistakable— it's Jane's. I read through her words cautiously at first, barely believing what I'm seeing, but as my eyes skim further down the page, my heart sinks with dread. What seems at first to be a joke soon turns into a horrific reality: Jane is completely serious about this.

According to the letter, Jane has met a special someone who lives on the mountain and she thinks she has fallen for him. Because of that, she has returned to him and will not be coming back for a while. She ends the letter by telling me not to worry, claiming that she is completely safe and fine.

It is unclear to me whether I should laugh or tear the paper to shreds. How could Jane say something like this and then ask me not to worry? What about her behavior suggests that she is fine? What part of this is normal? Definitely not the part where she meets some strange mountain-dwelling man, not the part where she claims to have fallen in love with him after being with him for what—half a day? And most definitely not the part where she thinks returning to be with him is a good idea. Or leaving me a letter in *her* apartment rather than call me, send me a text, hell, a letter by snail mail.

Clearly, Jane is in much worse condition than I thought.

"Oh, Jane," I say out loud. "What have you gone and done?"

Quickly, I head to my place to change from my working clothes into warm running gear, then pick up my coat, phone, and hiking shoes. I regret not going with Jane the first time she went on that run to make sure she was okay, and I hope I am not too late now. If Jane is in an unsafe situation, it is up to me to find her and bring her back home. Only God knows what kind of man she must have found in a strange place like that—most likely a cult leader.

Besides, after my run-ins with my abusive ex, I cannot think of a better time to get out of my comfort zone and go save a friend.

For now, I do not want to tell anyone or involve the authorities—not before I assess the situation and know what I am faced with. With a backpack behind me filled with essentials such as a water bottle, a flashlight, a knife (just in case), hiking gear and some sandwiches, I head out of my apartment and bike straight to the mountain.

I take every step with determination because I am all my best friend has. As the mountain comes into view, only one thought crosses my mind: "I am not coming back home without Jane."

BONUS SCENE

Can't get enough of Jane and Aldrick?
Grab the super steamy bonus scene
Click here to get started

Aurora and the Monster

Can't get enough Monsters of Mount Moorhead?
Read the first chapter of Sleeping Beauty Retelling–
Aurora and the Monster

urora

Scores of voices surrounded me like an uncomfortable embrace. I tried to open my eyes but my lids were heavy and the rest of me ached with a dull pain.

Somewhere near, loud pants carried to me on the wings of a hot breath and a huge presence loomed, casting darker shadows over me. Whoever it was smelled earthy and fresh.

Then, a touch, slimy and unpleasant. Full panic gripped my body while I struggled to wake up and react. Movement was impossible and everything hurt like hell. How long had I been asleep?

"Leave us now. Protect the door and let me take care of this little beauty," a rough, booming voice roared, sending a shiver down my spine.

Once more I tried to move and at last, I was able to raise my arms. My skin tingled with awareness. Someone, *something* foul was taking over my space and I needed to get up and run as far as my legs would take me...

Disoriented, my mind foggy, I attempted to take a few deep breaths. It was time for me to wake from this cruel dream.

"I should pierce your heart with a blade and end your life, little beauty, but the light inside me brightens when I look at you."

My heart pounded in my chest as I waited for my end, for there was no mistaking the meaning in his words. I didn't want to die like this, before I could inhale fresh air and see the world once again, before

I returned to smelling the roses on the castle grounds and go riding with Phillip, my beloved prince.

I fought to open my eyes so I could see the beast or man or whatever it was that stood in front of me, but the curse set upon me was keeping me chained to my state.

Just then, he pressed his lips to mine and I froze again. I tasted him, along with all the strength and passion that flowed from his body to mine.

Deep down I wanted to scream with rage, but he was suddenly devouring my lips, inhaling my scent, drawing out my soul—his energy connecting with mine.

Scorching heat rushed through my body, igniting my core, and my toes curled. How was this possible? The feeling was intense, arousing, and scandalous because I had no knowledge of this man who was devouring me. He was a stranger, a random visitor doing something that had been denied me for decades. Forbidden by a cruel fate.

When he finally stopped, I released a breath and at last, my eyelids fluttered, as if something about that kiss broke the last of the resistance within me that had kept me trapped in the darkness for so long.

At first, the whole world around me was barely visible in blurred tones. I moved my hands as I regained sensation in my limbs. The warmth I'd just felt on my lips suddenly moved down my chest, then my stomach and farther down to my core, making me gasp. I was not cold and numb anymore, but sentient, with heat flowing through me.

The image of my surroundings sharpened as my vision improved. I recognised everything—my chamber and my bed—but my memories were still very raw. I didn't even remember how I got here in the first place. My breaths were irregular and heavy, and my nightgown was stuck to my back.

"And she's awakened. That's a surprise," the same loud, rough voice spoke again and my head snapped instinctively to my right.

A giant of a man stood close, so close, staring down at me. He was bare-chested, muscular, and beautiful. Shock filled me at the sight, and my eyes felt like they were about to pop out of their sockets. His leather pants hung low on his hips, revealing a smattering of dark hairs on his torso. He was blond, his hair unkempt and long, but it was his eyes that drew me instantly to this stunning creature.

Fear washed over me like a tidal wave because I was certain that this man wasn't a normal human.

Indeed, he looked like a mutant ... some kind of beast. His purple eyes regarded me with purpose as if he was looking into my very soul. Flustered, I shook my head.

"What ... who are you? Where is Phillip? And my father ... the king?" I asked weakly, not recognising my own voice. My throat felt raw and sore. I wanted to remember so many details but my memories faded in and out.

I shuddered when he kept looking at me as though ready to consume me.

He smirked, tilting his head to the side. His gaze moved down to my lips, then my cleavage. I took a sharp inhale, feeling so exposed. He was bigger than any man I had ever seen. His muscular chest was enormous and a random thought hit me where I wondered how it would feel if he held me close. I wanted to touch my lips, as if that would help me confirm whether he'd been the one who kissed me and awakened me from my deep sleep.

"They are all dead. My men have killed everyone in the castle. Now it's just you and me, my Princess Aurora," he said, standing to his feet and looking impossibly large and menacing.

Dead. A whimper escaped me, but I couldn't

summon an ounce of grief. I was empty, drained, a shell without a past.

Once more I couldn't move, either because my muscles were stiff or because I was too afraid for my life. I could feel every ounce of this giant creature's power and more than anything, inexplicably, I wanted to be touched by his enormous arms and hands. Perhaps this scared me the most.

Despite the handsome face though, shadows of pain crept over his expression. What was his story and why was he here? Why was everyone dead? I couldn't even remember who those people were. My parents—I *knew* they'd existed yet not much of my life with them.

I shook my head in puzzlement. Or perhaps I simply didn't want his words to sink in. "No, you're lying to me. Phillip was here. He was the one who woke me up!" I shouted, remembering that other moment from the past.

Prince Phillip. I knew him—Phillip was safe ... familiar. I also knew who I was and I vaguely assumed the king and queen would probably be worried about me. Tears forced their way to my eyes, but I blinked to stop them from falling. I wasn't going to cry in front of this ... this brute. I didn't want to give him the satisfaction.

"Oh, princess, it seems you believe in fairytales, but the truth is that I was the one who woke you up. I came here to end your life, but instead I tasted your lips. I felt your arousal for me," he said, leaning closer and making me shiver.

Then, I caught movement at the periphery of my vision. A limb or something long and strange started to grow out of his body. At first I thought it could be a tail or another arm, but this would have been impossible. Then another one emerged, and another. Several tentacles came into view, appearing out of nowhere, sprouting from his flesh and gliding gracefully up and down like gentle waves.

I screamed in terror. "What are you? Stay away from me!" I shouted when one of the tentacles caressed my cheek, its texture wet and slimy. I pulled back in disgust but the beast laughed. I needed to run but my body refused to obey me and let me escape.

At least four tentacles had grown from each side, swirling like snakes in the air. I couldn't speak or breathe because then it occurred to me that this thing—this monster—had just kissed me.

"You ... you're ... don't touch me!" I shrieked.

"My name is Baadar and I'm your new king, little one. Stop lying to me. You were aroused by that kiss.

I could read your emotions like an open book," he hissed as one of his tentacles caressed my arm.

Still I wanted to get away from him, but my body kept failing me.

I frantically looked around, trying to figure out what to do. Was he really going to kill me?

"Never! You disgust me and you're never going to be my king!" My voice was scratchy, rising in pitch and breaking at the end.

I thrashed around on the bed as he held me captive, relieved I could at least do that, and the movement made my breasts bounce. His gaze roved over my body, pausing to take in my hardened nipples. I guessed my body didn't agree with my actions, even though I wouldn't ever admit it. I couldn't be all hot and bothered by this monster. This was insanity at best.

All of this had to be a product of my imagination. But then why did I feel so alive when his tentacles caressed my arm? When he'd kissed me before? I panted as he stared at me with a hunger and thirst for all that was forbidden.

Then, one of his tentacles shot outward and wrapped itself around my waist. My gown was so thin and I only just then realized I was wearing nothing underneath. I couldn't even remember why or if my maid had helped me change or whether I'd dressed myself.

"Don't lie to me, human. I haven't decided yet what I am going to do with you but look how wet you are for your master. Your scent is driving me mad and I'm thirsty for your blood, too," he growled, his huge tentacles lifting me off the bed and slamming me against the wall.

The impact drew a scream of pain from me. This was it. Soon, I'd be taking my last breath. Phillip was never going to rescue me from this monster because he was dead.

His piercing purple eyes bore into mine as he approached me. I smelled the earthiness of his flesh that reminded me of balmy summer nights. I lost all sense of time as his huge body crashed into mine, violently and possessively. His hard muscles pressed against me while his beautiful mouth was only inches from mine.

I wanted to turn my head and look away but found myself unable to, rooted to the spot as I was, mesmerized by his eyes.

Then, something hard and big poked me between my legs.

"So beautiful ... and you smell divine when you're scared, my princess. It would be such a shame to slit your throat just now." He leaned closer and sniffed me, then reached out to move a stray lock of hair away from my flustered face. As much as I tried to stop it, scorching heat rushed through me and desire muddled my head. I hated feeling this way for a vile creature like this.

But all thought was sucked away from my brain when a ridged, yet oddly smooth, wet tentacle moved over my backside, then slid right between my legs.

"For the love of—" I wheezed, my words stopping because I couldn't speak. When the thing brushed over my sex, I wanted to yell out my pleasure and it took everything I had in me to hold that back. My body trembled, out of control, radiating with energy. I bit my bottom lip, once more tamping down a cry of ecstasy.

"You won't deceive me, princess," he muttered. "Just one more kiss. One more, before I kill you."

And then he pressed his lips to mine in a mind-blowing, explosive and urgent kiss while his tentacle rubbed itself over my clit. I moaned into his mouth as this was all too much. The pressure between my legs was unbearable and his lips tasted like ambrosia, earth and sun.

He kissed me like the monster he was, as though

he'd never tasted a human woman before—yearning and desperate. My body made all the decisions as I opened up to him, parting my lips and allowing his tongue to caress mine. His mouth was suddenly everywhere, hard and demanding.

This was better than the first time and I was soaked for him. My juices gushed down my leg as his probing tentacle continued to violate me.

"Tell me, my princess, do you want me to touch you down there and lick your precious cum off your thigh?" he asked, ending the kiss. He, too, seemed to struggle with his breathing.

His tentacle retracted and I was suddenly disappointed it wasn't touching me anymore. I must have lost my mind.

My chest rose and fell in rapid movements as I stared at him, hardly believing my eyes as I tried to gather my wits, tried to understand ... how could I want more?

"Let me go. I hate you," I spat, and he smirked in reaction.

Kneeling in front of me, he forced my legs apart.

"Wrong answer," he murmured before everything went dark again.

Printed in Great Britain
by Amazon

22946370R00109